Hugh walking into the office, dark and fabulously handsome and livid with anger because Paul was kissing her. Hugh sitting beside her on the stairs after she had fallen. Hugh lifting her in his arms to carry her out to his car...

Memory took Lissa back as far as that. Then her mind wasn't working at all. Only her body was functioning and her body was giving her all sorts of unfamiliar, disturbing messages.

LIGHTNING STRIKE

BY

MARJORIE LEWTY

MILLS & BOON LIMITED
ETON HOUSE   18-24 PARADISE ROAD
RICHMOND   SURREY   TW9 1SR

*First published in Great Britain 1990
by Mills & Boon Limited*

© Marjorie Lewty 1990

*Australian copyright 1990
Philippine copyright 1990
This edition 1990*

ISBN 0 263 76898 8

*Set in Times Roman 11 on 12 pt.
01-9012-51040 C*

Made and printed in Great Britain

CHAPTER ONE

THE kiss took Lissa completely by surprise. No way had she invited it, and she certainly wasn't enjoying it.

The office Lissa shared with Paul Donaldson, Winchester's sales director, was divided from the spacious, open-plan main office by a glass partition. And tonight, at six twenty-five, everyone except Lissa and Paul had already left. The lights over the work-stations were out, the typewriters and computers were shrouded in their silver-grey plastic covers. The only sound was the rumble of traffic from the London street below and the soft ticking of the quartz clocks, one at each end of the long room.

Lissa had been bending over her desk, checking that everything she would need for the fortnight's marketing trip to Scotland was packed away in her briefcase. Her travelling bag had already been put in Paul's car—she had handed it over to him when she'd arrived at the office this morning. As soon as they were both ready they would start on their car journey north, taking turns with the driving.

As she clipped the fastening of her briefcase, a pleasant sense of excitement had bubbled inside her, sending an extra sparkle to green eyes beneath their silky, curving lashes. She had been looking forward to the trip—it would be her first assignment as Paul Donaldson's PA and it would be splendid experience. She'd never been to Scotland and that had been a plus. And to make everything even better the timing had fitted in so well with plans at home.

Suddenly, as she'd straightened up, a pair of arms had come round her from behind. She hadn't heard Paul come across from his own desk. In the few weeks she'd been working for him he'd never made anything approaching a pass at her, but now the pressure of those warm hands, just below the swell of her breasts, was distinctly purposeful.

She gave a little gasp and tried to pull away, but his hands slid upwards and moulded her breasts. She felt the heat of them through the thin stuff of her silky blouse. His mouth nuzzled into the back of her neck, under the chestnut curls which she always tied back demurely in the office.

'Paul—please...' She told herself hastily that this wasn't a threatening situation, Paul wasn't that kind of man.

'You're so damn pretty.' His voice was muffled by her hair. 'I've been wanting to do this for ages, and now we're going to be on our own we'll have lots of fun, won't we?' He swung her neatly round in his arms, laughing, until their faces were only inches apart.

'No, Paul, this really isn't on...' she protested indignantly.

Paul's handsome face loomed close above hers. She could smell the mixture of drinks on his breath—he'd had a very long lunch-hour today. She could see the red colour spreading over his cheekbones, the pulse that beat at his temple below his floppy fairish hair, his mouth coming nearer and nearer until his open lips fastened on hers.

They were alone in the office—probably alone in the whole building except for the caretaker on the ground floor. Anger, rather than fear, gripped Lissa's stomach. Her arms were squashed against her body but she managed to bend them at the elbow and raise her hands to Paul's shoulders to try to push him away. It was hopeless—like pushing against a rock.

'What the hell's going on here?' A man's voice, deep and furious, came from the direction of the door into the corridor, and Lissa felt herself released so promptly that she nearly fell over.

Paul reacted with incredible speed. He straightened his tie and produced his rueful, charming smile. 'Hugh! Well, well! You've chosen an inopportune moment for your return, haven't you?'

'That's a matter of opinion.' The newcomer bit the words out as he came towards them, his dark, lean face hard as granite.

Lissa backed against her desk, her dazed eyes on the man who had just appeared. Hugh Winchester—the managing director. He was rather a remote figure to Lissa—all she knew about him was that he was Paul's stepbrother, but Paul had only mentioned him once to her. Then he had said, with his wry grin, 'Not really my cup of tea. Too clever by half—a mind like a razor-blade.'

Hugh Winchester seemed to be away from the office a great deal of the time. Lissa had only seen him in the distance and had never spoken to him. But now, close up, he was much larger than she had imagined. Large, and dark as night, and quite terrifying in the cold anger he was obviously keeping under strict control.

He didn't even glance at her. 'Shall we go up to my office, Paul? There are one or two things we have to discuss. If you're not too busy, that is.' His voice was icy with contempt.

Paul gave an embarrassed laugh. 'Surely you don't imagine——'

'That's just it,' the other man interrupted. 'At this moment my imagination's working overtime.' He nodded implacably towards the open doorway that led to the corridor.

'Oh, all right, *be* like that, then,' Paul said sulkily. He lifted his eyebrows in Lissa's direction, shrugged, and sauntered away towards the lift, keeping up a show of nonchalance.

Hugh Winchester strode after him, but at the door he turned and came back to Lissa.

Her heart thumped uncomfortably. He wasn't going to read her a lecture, surely? Because if he was, she wasn't going to put up with——

'Miss Stephens, isn't it?' he said curtly. 'I understand from Mrs Henderson that there were plans for you to drive up to Scotland with my stepbrother tonight. I may as well tell you now that you won't be needed there.'

Her head went back to meet eyes that were a strange shade of light grey, with a darker rim round the iris. They were totally devoid of expression and under the fluorescent lighting they shone like polished steel.

'Not needed? But it was all settled. I've made arrangements . . .' He couldn't just walk in like this and disrupt all the plans that had been made days ago.

'Then you'll just have to unmake them, won't you?' There was a nasty edge to his voice. 'There will no doubt be other opportunities for fun and games—outside office hours.' Cold grey eyes raked her from head to foot. Thin lips curled ironically.

She couldn't speak. The words of denial choked in her throat. What a beastly, hateful man! She had to get away from him. Grabbing her handbag from her desk she rushed out of the office, her knees shaking, and stumbled up two flights of stairs to the women's cloakroom, where she sank on to a stool, trembling with rage. Nobody had ever spoken to her like that before. Nobody. He was the most odious man she had ever met. Even if he was the managing director he had no right to treat his staff in that arrogant, high-handed way.

The managing director himself evidently thought otherwise. In his office on the top floor of the building he stood towering over his handsome young stepbrother, who was perched on the edge of a large desk, swinging one elegantly trousered leg.

'Aren't you rather overdoing the Big Brother act, Hugh? There wasn't any reason——'

'Reason! You must let me be the judge of that. I met Mrs Henderson on the way home and she tackled me. She *supposed* it was all right, your taking Miss Stephens with you to Scotland, but the girl had only been with the company a very short time and she was *very* young. And *very* pretty...' His lips twisted as he imitated the company secretary's worried voice. 'I got the message—Mrs Henderson knows you and she knows the score. It's bloody humiliating when one's own stepbrother has a reputation in the company for seducing the young girls on the staff.'

'Oh, come on, Hugh,' Paul bridled defensively. 'We're not all plaster saints like you, but I didn't intend to *seduce* Lissa Stephens, as you so delicately put it. What you saw downstairs was simply a kiss at the end of the day's work. Nothing very terrible about that, surely?'

Hugh Winchester frowned, and his hands, hanging loosely by his sides, curled tensely before they relaxed again. 'Perhaps not, but it's what a kiss leads to. And when you intend to spend a fortnight in Scotland with a girl, it's reasonable to deduce what the situation would be at the end of the fortnight.'

'Reasonable for you, no doubt.' Paul's fair cheeks were crimson as he slipped off the desk and confronted the much taller man. 'Everything's logical cause-and-effect with you. Feelings don't enter into it. You wouldn't kiss a girl goodnight, would you? You'd kiss your computer.'

The other man ignored the jibe. 'As I see it,' he said grimly, 'you've already been the cause of too many unfortunate effects in this company, Paul. You know damn well that if you weren't my stepbrother you'd be out on your ear by now.'

Paul glared defiantly. 'I suppose you mean Carolyn? Come on, Hugh, you can't still hold that against me? It's all in the past now.'

'In your past, you mean. Not in mine. I'm the one who's left holding the baby. And that damn near happened literally,' he added crudely.

Paul stuck his hands in his pockets, turning away. 'I fixed it all up, I didn't let Carolyn down, you know that. If you like to play Old Daddy Longlegs to the girl now, that's your lookout. Anyway, it wasn't all my fault, Carolyn was only too——'

'Shut up!' his stepbrother roared suddenly, and Paul's face went ashen. 'Shut up and get out of my sight. Go off on your Scottish trip and don't, for heaven's sake, let me see your face again for a long time. Go on, get out.'

Paul went.

In the girls' cloakroom Lissa stared at her white face in the mirror. What a beastly thing to happen, and how could Paul make such a fool of himself—and of her? It was the very last thing she'd expected.

One of the things that Lissa particularly appreciated about working in the London office of Winchester Electronics and Office Equipment was that the modern, airy, open-plan design didn't lend itself to what was known as sexual harassment. Her father, whose opinion on business matters she valued, always held that an office was a place to work in and not to fool about in. And Lissa, being career-minded, cheerfully agreed with him.

So she had been happy to join Winchester, after several dead-end jobs, finishing with a brief spell in the office of a wholesale electric-supply company, where the male staff had rapidly become much too friendly towards an eye-catching young lady with sea-green eyes and rather spectacular chestnut curls.

She'd enjoyed working with Paul during the few weeks she'd been his PA. He was the easiest man in the world to work with, always had a grin and a light word when things got hectic in the office.

Oh, yes, they'd got on well and Lissa had had no grumbles about standing in for him when he'd wanted to take the day off to drive one of his girl-friends down to the coast; or about scouring the shops in her lunch-hour for a birthday present for another lovely lady; or booking theatre seats, res-taurant tables, ordering flowers. She'd known he was an incorrigible flirt, but it had all seemed so harmless. They'd laughed together about his girl-friends. She'd *liked* Paul.

The one thing she'd never expected was that he'd make a pass at *her*. But it had only been because he'd had too much to drink at lunch, she was sure it was. And then—how desperately unlucky that Hugh Winchester should have walked in at that moment and put his veto on her trip to Scotland with Paul. She *could* have handled Paul and his sudden flirtatious attitude, she was sure she could. There had been absolutely no need for that horrible man to over-react as he had done.

She swilled her face with cool water and tried to bring her usual common sense to bear on what she was going to do. She couldn't go home—the American family would be in residence there by now—so where could she go tonight? A hotel? That was the only solution. With sudden horror, she re-alised that her travelling case was in Paul's car. She wouldn't be able to book into a hotel without lug-gage. She grabbed her coat from her locker, picked up her handbag and dashed out to the lift. She must get down to the garage and rescue her case before Paul left.

She pressed the lift button. Nothing happened. Of course—the lift *would* have stopped working for the night, wouldn't it? Cursing under her breath, seething with annoyance, Lissa launched herself down four flights of stairs.

It was on the very bottom bend that the worst happened. The carpeted staircase was like a ski slalom—she'd been turning and twisting so fast that she lost control on the final bend. As she rounded the corner it was as if the wall ahead came up to meet her. Her feet slipped on the thick carpet and she slithered downwards to fall awkwardly on to the third step from the bottom. For a moment she lay quite still, wondering if she'd broken any bones. That would just be the end, she thought, and stupid tears welled up behind her eyelids. She wasn't a weepy girl, but everything had just got too much for her.

'Having fun?' Hugh Winchester's deep voice, heavy with irony, came from behind as he caught up with her on his way down.

Lissa couldn't have replied if her life had depended on it. She dragged herself into a sitting position, keeping her eyes lowered. They encountered a pair of immaculate black shoes.

'What happened? You're not hurt, are you?'

You wouldn't care if I'd broken my neck, Lissa thought venomously. She shook her head dumbly. Go away, she willed him. Get out of my sight.

The shoes moved downwards and their owner lowered himself to sit on the stair beside her.

'*Are* you hurt?' he repeated and there was more than a hint of impatience in his voice.

She didn't know whether she was hurt or not but she shook her head again, biting her lower lip hard.

A hand came out and tipped back her chin.

'You're crying,' Hugh Winchester said in an accusing, exasperated voice. 'Is it such a terrible blow to have your trip with Paul cancelled? Whatever's been going on between you, I can tell you that my charming young stepbrother is poison for a little girl like you, you know. He's not worth your tears.'

Little girl! *Ooh!* Fury dried up Lissa's tears immediately. Not for the first time, she regretted that she looked much younger than her twenty-two years. 'Whatever you're insinuating about Paul and me, it's not true. There's nothing "going on" between us. Absolutely nothing.'

'No? That wasn't how it looked when I walked in just now.'

Lissa's anger boiled over. 'I can't help how it *looked* to someone with a mind like yours,' she flung at him. 'That's the way it *is*.'

For a long moment they glared at each other, angry green eyes meeting chilly grey ones, and Lissa felt a sharp squeeze of something like fear in the pit of her stomach. But she didn't care, at that moment, if he *was* the head of the company; she didn't care if he sacked her. She hated unfairness and being misjudged—it was one of the few things that roused her temper.

When her gaze didn't waver he shrugged. 'OK, if you say so, but you're still not going to Scotland with him. Now I suggest you take yourself home.'

He got to his feet, holding out a hand to help her up.

She ignored his hand and pushed against the carpet to lever herself up. Then she sat down again—hard. Damn! She *had* injured herself somewhere. She tried again, with the same result, and was aware of a sharp pain in her right knee. Grasping the hand-rail, she managed to pull herself up, keeping the weight on her left leg. Oh, lord, she thought desperately, it only needed this!

The man sighed heavily, sizing up the situation. 'Sit down again, and let's find out what the damage is,' he ordered, and Lissa had no choice but to obey. He knelt in front of her, flexing her ankles, then her knees. As he reached the right knee she let out a little yelp.

'Hm, could be anything,' he said. 'Pulled muscle, torn tendon, even a fracture—though I hope not. At all events, you need to see a doctor. I'd better take you home.'

'No,' said Lissa sharply, and added rather reluctantly, 'thank you. I can't—I'm not going home.'

He gave her a hard look. 'It's no use hanging around here, my girl. Paul's already left.'

Lissa wanted to scream or hit out at him. In spite of what she'd said he really *did* believe she was breaking her heart about not going to Scotland with Paul. With difficulty she controlled her resentment. She said tightly, 'At the moment I'm not interested in Paul's whereabouts. All that interests me is that my travelling bag is in his car. I propose to spend the night in a hotel, so I need my luggage.'

Seeing the dark brows go up, she felt a small sense of triumph. At least she had surprised him. She congratulated herself on being able to speak so lucidly, after all that had happened.

He sat down again beside her. She wished he wouldn't—there was something decidedly un-nerving about the hard, masculine body at such close quarters. He wasn't actually touching her, of course, but she was disturbingly aware of the mus-cular frame beneath the expensively tailored char-coal suit. Aware in a way she'd never been aware of Paul, not even when he'd pounced on her just now.

'Look,' he said, with studied patience, 'suppose you tell me what you're talking about. Why can't you go home, and what's all this damn silly stuff about a hotel? Of course you can't go to a hotel, not until you've seen a doctor, anyway.'

Two can play at being patronising, Lissa thought, and she said calmly, spacing out the words as if she were explaining to a not-over-bright third-former, 'I can't go home because my home is occupied by an American family with five children. My parents arranged a holiday house-exchange and they are at present somewhere in Florida. I haven't any rela-tives nearer than Cornwall and no particular friends I can park myself on in London—especially with a damaged knee. A hotel seems the only solution so I'll be grateful if you'll find out whether Paul has taken my case out of his car and left it somewhere.' Her chestnut curls, which had come loose from their ribbon, bounced as she turned her head away with a lofty gesture, and prepared to wait.

'Oh, lord.' Hugh Winchester clicked his tongue. 'Worse and worse. OK, stay here and I'll go down to the garage and have a look for it.'

He was back very quickly—with no case. At the expression on Lissa's face he said, 'Don't panic, I've found your case. Paul must have chucked it out of his car—it landed in a small puddle, I'm afraid, but I'm sure that wouldn't worry my step-brother unduly. I've brought my car round to the side—you'd better come to my place and I'll get a doctor friend of mine to take a look at you.'

Lissa lifted her chin. 'Really, there's no need to trouble you. Perhaps if you could take me to a hospital ...' She pulled herself up to demonstrate that she wasn't totally helpless and winced with the sudden pain in her knee.

'Don't be a silly child,' Hugh Winchester said impatiently. 'A hospital won't keep you in overnight if it turns out to be nothing more dramatic than a strained knee—and then where will you be? Scouring London to find a hotel room, with the city full of tourists? Of course I'll see you right. Anyway,' he added, frowning, 'if there's some fault in the staircase I'm responsible as head of the firm.'

'You needn't worry, I shan't sue for damages.' Lissa tried to look dignified, but it wasn't easy when she was standing on one leg, hanging on to the hand-rail. 'If you want to know the cause of the accident, you can find it in the treatment I'd just received from the company's directors—both of them,' she added pointedly. 'I couldn't get away fast enough.'

Hugh Winchester was really looking at her now—as if she was a human being and not some minor vexation that had been wished on him by a stroke of malignant fate. 'I—see,' he said slowly. And then, more rapidly, 'Well, if that's the case, it's the

clear duty of the guilty parties to take charge of
you, and, as my stepbrother has already left, I'm
afraid you'll have to put up with me. Come along,
let me give you a lift to the car.'

'No,' squeaked Lissa as his arms went round her.
'I can——'

'No, you can't,' he said, and lifted her easily.

She was held fast against him, her curls spreading
in a cloud over his charcoal jacket, her cheek
anchored to his chest. She could hear the firm, even
beat of his heart, smell the clean, masculine smell
of him. And suddenly, from somewhere in the un-
conscious depths of her, came the astonishing sense
that this was natural and—and *right*. For a split
second she felt herself press even nearer to him and
of their own accord her hands linked themselves
behind his neck.

'That's right, infant, hang on, we're nearly there.'

Common sense returned like a cold slap in the
face. How pathetic could you get? Why, the man
was a patronising, arrogant—bully. *Infant* indeed!

He must have contacted the caretaker, Jenner,
for the man was waiting at the back door of the
building, outside which a sleek, dark red Jaguar
was parked.

'Slid down them stairs, did you, miss? Nasty,
dangerous stuff, that carpet.' Jenner cast a sideways look at the managing director.

'I agree with you, Jenner,' the managing director
said suavely. 'It must be replaced as soon as possible. Now, if you could just hold the car door wide
open for me while I help Miss Stephens inside...'
He lowered Lissa on to her good leg. 'There you

are then, hop in,' he said, and added with a faint grin, 'Literally, I mean.'

Amazing—the man had a sense of humour! That was something she herself was going to need a plentiful supply of in the very near future. She eased herself into the front seat, drawing in a quick breath as the pain in her knee stabbed viciously.

'Bad?' Hugh Winchester asked, as he got in beside her. She would have appreciated a word of sympathy but none was forthcoming. Paul would have been sympathetic; he was always thoughtful if she had a cold or a headache.

'Only for a moment.' She settled back with a sigh of relief and reached for the seatbelt. 'I'm sure it's nothing much.'

'We'll see,' he said curtly.

She stole a glance at his uncompromising profile as he started the engine. Oh, well, she couldn't expect sympathy, could she? She was nothing but a nuisance to him. For the first time she realised, with a sinking heart, that her job was very probably at stake after all this. Just when she was hoping to get on in the company—possibly even exchange a secretarial job for training on the technical side of computing—a prospect which had always appealed to her. She mustn't put that at risk by getting any further on the wrong side of the managing director than she had done already. She thought quickly and decided that for the moment the intelligent thing was to knuckle under and submit to his patronising, authoritarian attitude.

She folded her hands and murmured meekly, 'It's very kind of you to bother with me, Mr Winchester.'

He slid her a quick glance that might have been cynical. 'Not at all,' he said stiffly.

Dusk was falling over the city on this April evening. Lissa relapsed into silence as the big car snaked its way along the London streets, and she found herself almost enjoying the novelty of being ferried round town in such luxury. The car smelt rather delightfully of new leather, with a faint whiff of cigar smoke. Typical managing director stuff, she thought, like everything else about the man— his immaculately tailored charcoal suit, the correct rim of snowy shirt showing beneath his cuff, the glint of steel—platinum?—from the square watch half hidden against the short black hairs of his wrist. Most of all his super-confident, not to say overbearing attitude.

She glanced at his hands as they lay relaxed on the wheel, the fingers long and sinewy, the short-cut nails manicured, and again she felt that twinge of something like fear in the pit of her stomach. Oh, yes, quite a lad was our Mr Winchester, she thought, with an effort to reduce him to size in her own mind.

He finally brought the car to rest outside a large, purpose-built block of flats somewhere in the West End. 'Good, we can park here for the moment while we get you inside.'

He got out and fed the meter, and then opened Lissa's door and held out both his hands. 'Take it easy,' he said. 'You don't want to aggravate that strain.'

You mean *you* don't want me to, Lissa almost giggled. I bet you don't. Obediently she allowed him to help her out, and she couldn't deny that it

was comforting to feel the tautness of his body as
she leaned against him to limp across the pavement
and into the lobby of the building. Comforting—
and something else! The twinge in her stomach
suddenly became much more definite—a sort of
lurching feeling that owed nothing to the fact that
they were swooping upwards in a lift.

It was humiliating that a man she so disliked
should have the power to turn her on so immediately! She supposed that he *was* a very sexy man—
if you liked that kind of dark, brooding mascu-
linity—which she didn't. She was far more at home
with Paul's cheerful, teasing approach—at least she
had been until that unexpectedly torrid scene in the
office just now. Oh, dear, how difficult this man-
woman thing was! You never knew where you were
with the brutes.

The apartment was more or less what she had
expected—squashy pale leather chairs, built-in
cupboards, low tables with smoked-glass tops. Like
an executive reception suite, Lissa thought, and just
about as warm and welcoming.

Hugh Winchester lowered her on to a wide sofa,
arranged a plum-coloured velvet cushion at her
back and said, 'You'd better put your feet up. Shall
I help?'

He didn't wait for an answer. He lifted her left
leg and then, quite gently, the damaged right one.
Lissa bit her lip hard. 'Did that hurt much?' he
said. His hand was still encircling her ankle.

She nodded, biting her lip. 'A little.'

'Pull up your skirt,' he said.

Her eyes widened and colour flooded into her
cheeks. 'What...?'

He clicked his tongue impatiently. 'I want to see the damage for myself—no ulterior motive.'

Of course! He *would* enjoy making her look a fool. But she had decided not to fight him—not at this moment, anyway. Obediently she pulled up her slim navy skirt and felt his hand gently touch her leg. Was it necessary for him to let his hand linger quite so long, or to stroke the silk-covered knee quite so assiduously? Lissa felt the warmth in her cheeks beginning to turn to a burning heat. It was one thing to have a doctor examine you, quite another to——

'Hm.' He removed his hand and pulled down her skirt. 'It seems badly swollen. I'll get on the phone to John and see if he can come round and take a look at it. Meanwhile, would you like a drink? A drop of brandy would help to pull you together after the shock.'

'Just a glass of water, please,' Lissa said politely. After *which* shock? she wondered—there had been several.

He went over to a drinks cupboard and brought her bottled spring water in a crystal glass. He mixed a drink for himself and carried it across to one of the deep leather chairs, picking up a cordless phone on the way. Here he sank down, spreading his long legs in front of him, with a weary sigh. He could hardly have made it more plain that he'd had a busy day and she was being a horrible nuisance.

When he'd taken a long swig of his drink he pulled out the phone's small aerial and dialled. 'John? Hugh here—fine, thanks, and you? Good. Look, John, I'm at home and I've got a young girl from the office here with a damaged knee. She took a tumble on the office stairs and I feel somewhat responsible. Could you possibly...? Oh, good, thanks, pal. See you in a few minutes, then.'

He drained his glass and put it down, with the phone, on the floor beside his chair. Then, without another word to Lissa, he lay back and closed his eyes.

Lissa sipped the cool water and almost wished she'd asked for brandy. She was beginning to feel very much the worse for wear and her knee was throbbing painfully. Oh, if only she could have gone home! Then she could have crawled into bed with a couple of aspirins and phoned for her own doctor in the morning, and not been dependent on any-one—least of all on this disgustingly superior in-dividual who spoiled her plans, ordered her about, and treated her like a thorn in his flesh.

She could only hope this doctor was a human being and that he'd suggest some way out for her. Perhaps a stay overnight in a nursing home? Only she didn't have enough money to pay for that.

She looked at the man sprawled in the chair op-posite. He seemed to be asleep. He really did look fagged out, she had to admit; perhaps he'd been travelling all day. Her lips softened as she watched the way his broad chest rose and fell with slow, even breathing. The strange grey eyes were hooded under their heavy lids, the long lashes resting on his lean cheeks. One lock of dark hair hung over his wide forehead where tiny lines were just beginning to form, creasing the smooth, tanned skin.

No, thought Lissa quite violently, she was *not* going to allow herself to feel sympathy for the man. He had only himself to blame for being saddled with her. If he hadn't interfered so high-handedly and so unnecessarily with the plans for Paul to take her to Scotland with him, none of this would have happened. It served him right!

But resentment didn't help her, of course, and, moving her leg slightly to try to ease the pain in her knee, Lissa firmed her pretty mouth and settled down to wait for the next unpleasant thing to happen on this disastrous evening.

CHAPTER TWO

TEN minutes later a buzzer sounded from across the room, near the door. The man in the chair opposite Lissa didn't stir.

'Mr Winchester,' she said softly. Then, louder, 'Mr Winchester, there's someone at the door.'

No response. Twisting her left leg off the sofa, she leaned across and poked him at the nearest spot, which was just below the belt of his trousers.

He shot up then. 'What the...?' He looked positively outraged.

Lissa couldn't help grinning. 'Someone at the door,' she said again.

'Oh.' He heaved himself out of the chair and went over to the intercom. 'Hello—John? OK, come on up.'

He shot a nasty look at Lissa and went out to the corridor. Her grin widened and she wished she'd poked him even harder. It did something for her self-esteem to have awakened the dictatorial managing director of Winchester's in such an undignified fashion.

He was back presently with a youngish man, small and fair, with twinkling eyes behind gold-rimmed glasses.

'This is the girl I told you about, John.' Hugh Winchester nodded towards the sofa.

How was *that* for a courteous introduction, then? 'My name's Lissa Stephens, Doctor,' she volunteered rather pointedly, smiling as the young man approached.

He sat on the edge of the sofa and smiled back. 'Hello, Miss Stephens, I'm John Fraser. Delighted to meet you.' He looked delighted too. 'But sorry to hear you've been throwing yourself down the stairs. Did Hugh tire you, working overtime? He's a demon for work.'

'Oh, nothing like that,' Lissa murmured. 'It was my own fault entirely. Mr Winchester happened to be there at the time and felt he ought to rescue me. I've been a terrible nuisance to him, I'm afraid.' She pushed back her cloud of tawny hair and a dimple appeared in her left cheek.

'I can't believe that,' the doctor said gallantly. He slid a glance towards his friend, who had retired to the other side of the room and was glancing through a journal. The doctor shrugged. 'Oh, well—let's see the damage.'

The examination was thorough and gentle. At the end of it the doctor stood up and said, 'No fracture, I'm pretty sure of that. The trouble's in a tendon and the cure for that is rest. Four or five days immobilised should do the trick—then go easy with getting around. Cold compress for the swelling.'

Lissa bit her lip. 'But I can't——' she began, and Hugh interrupted.

'Miss Stephens has a slight difficulty,' he said. 'To put it in a nutshell, for various reasons she finds herself homeless at the moment. She'd been on her way north on a business trip when the accident occurred.' He threw a hunted look round the large room. 'I can't keep her here,' he said.

The doctor chuckled. 'I don't exactly see you as a nursing auxiliary, old boy. But there's no problem—we've got a room free at Doverscourt for a few days—a postponed op.' He turned to Lissa to add, 'Doverscourt is a nursing home just round the corner, Miss Stephens. I'm on the staff there, and I'm sure they will make you most comfortable.'

A West End nursing home! Hundreds of pounds a night probably!

'I'm afraid I couldn't——' she began.

'That's an excellent idea.' Hugh Winchester fairly jumped at it. 'My responsibility, of course.'

The matter was taken out of Lissa's hands. 'We'll help Miss Stephens into your car and take her round there straight away.' Dr Fraser was firmly professional. 'The sooner she's in bed and being treated for that swelling, the better. And they can take an X-ray to check up on any possible fracture.'

'Good,' said Hugh Winchester crisply, and Lissa felt like a parcel that had been wrongly delivered as she was helped out to the car.

Five days later Lissa sat in a cushioned chair beside her bed, wrapped in a flower-patterned nylon gown over her nightdress, and decided that being ill was a very pleasant experience—if you had the money.

Everything about Doverscourt Nursing Home was soaked in luxury. The patient's every need, even every whim, was pandered to. The food was heavenly; the chef himself visited each room in the morning to discuss the day's cuisine. The staff were cool, efficient, friendly. Colour TV, stereo, radio, telephone—all laid on.

Except for a bunch of cream rosebuds with a card saying, 'Get well soon, HW', Lissa had not seen or heard anything from High Winchester. The flowers had evidently been ordered by phone, for the message was written in a round, artless hand that was certainly not the managing director's. Lissa told herself that it was all she could expect; Hugh Winchester wasn't the kind of man to treat this unfortunate incident as in any way personal. His doctor friend, John Fraser, however, called each day and seemed to have time to stay for a chat.

He had enquired about her taste in reading and next day had arrived with a stack of paperbacks, historical romances and detective mysteries, which she had devoured eagerly. She had phoned her parents in Florida and given them the news, making reassuring noises when her mother had jabbered with anxiety. She was recovering quickly, she'd told them, and would probably join the Scottish trip, as arranged, in a day or two.

That was a lie, of course; she knew perfectly well that she wouldn't be going to Scotland. The Winchester man had made that clear and in the company his word was law. She had become so lulled by the atmosphere of Doverscourt that she didn't worry much about it—or anything else. She simply lay back and relaxed, which was what she was encouraged to do—except for wiggling her toes to keep the muscles of her legs in trim.

Rather too often for her peace of mind she let her eyes rest on the cream rosebuds and then, of course, she thought about Hugh Winchester. He was a puzzle. She simply couldn't understand why he had taken the responsibility for her accident so seriously. Any other man, in similar circumstances, she felt, would have simply dumped her at a hospital and washed his hands of the whole matter.

It couldn't be, could it, that he'd taken a sudden liking to her? Reading Regency romances put ideas into your head. And lying in bed, surrounded by luxury, was all too conducive to dreaming up impossible fantasies. Hugh Winchester, she thought, was a little like one of those stiff, arrogant Regency heroes.

She had to remind herself that he hadn't shown the slightest sign of being impressed—entirely the reverse. He'd considered her a silly young thing with not enough intelligence to see through Paul Donaldson or to avoid hurling herself down the staircase. Any other explanation was just—well, not exactly wishful thinking. Just a waste of time.

No, the only explanation was that he was really worried that she would sue the firm for her accident on the stairs. Ah, well, she would probably not see him again when she left the nursing home.

In that she was quite wrong, for later that morning her young nurse, rather more pink-cheeked than usual, came in to announce a visitor, and the managing director himself appeared behind her in the doorway, looking, Lissa had to admit, quite gorgeous in the obligatory dark suit and white shirt of the senior executive.

He sauntered across the room and perched on the edge of the bed, regarding her with a steady gaze that made her lower her eyes quickly. 'Hello, how goes it? John says you're ready to be released from bondage tomorrow if you take it easy. It seems a bit early to me, but apparently they need the room. How do you feel about it?'

Lissa found that her heart was beating uncomfortably fast. Suddenly the room seemed full of his masculine presence—the very air was vibrating with it.

She threw a small smile roughly in his direction, without meeting his eyes. 'I've been walking around yesterday and today and I'm quite ready to get along under my own steam. Although I must confess I've rather enjoyed being spoiled. Thank you for the roses, by the way.'

'Not at all,' he said, and then there was silence.

Lissa broke into it quickly. 'About paying for the room—perhaps if you could arrange that and I'll repay you when my parents come home. My own bank account's rather low at the moment.'

He waved a hand dismissively. 'Don't let me hear another word about that. It's all taken care of. And I don't expect thanks, either. I don't know who had that damned slippery carpet put down on the stairs in my absence, but certainly the firm must take the responsibility for your accident. I'm only glad it wasn't any worse.'

She opened her mouth to demur but he went straight on, 'Now—if you're being discharged tomorrow, have you made any plans about where you will go? I take it you still can't go back to your own home?'

'I shall go to my cousin's,' she said, trying to sound as if she had fixed it all up, whereas she had only just this minute thought of it. 'She has a small hotel in Marazion, near Penzance, and she won't be full up in April.'

He frowned. 'Penzance—at the very tip of Cornwall! Do you really have to travel all the way out there on your own? I hardly think you're up to it yet, you know.'

'I can't think of anywhere else,' Lissa told him. 'I can stay there for a few more days until I'm ready to come back to work.' She glanced quickly at him and away again. Was he going to say that her job was at an end?

'Ye-es,' he said thoughtfully. 'We'll have to think that one out. After what's happened there's no question of your working with Paul again.'

'Oh, but surely——?' she began.

He held up a hand. '*No.*'

Lissa's lips firmed mutinously, but she had already found that arguing with him was a waste of time.

'Have you been in touch with your cousin?' he rapped out, and she saw that he was angry. Anything to do with Paul seemed to annoy him. The stepbrothers obviously didn't hit it off.

'Well—er—no, not yet.'

'Then don't. I have a better idea.'

The time had come for Lissa to assert herself. 'Look,' she said. 'There is absolutely no need for you to bother with me any longer. I'm not an invalid now, I can get along under my own steam. And——' she tossed back her riot of tawny curls '—I prefer to do that.'

He went on as if she hadn't spoken. 'How much computing work have you done since you've been with Paul?'

The way he shot the question out took her off guard. 'Computing work? Why, none at all. It wasn't needed in our department,' she said blankly. 'Should I have done?'

'Not even word-processing?'

'No. Paul intended to get one put in. I kept reminding him because it seemed a bit silly that I should still be working on an ordinary typewriter, but somehow he never got around to it.'

Hugh Winchester's lips compressed. 'That doesn't surprise me. Well, how do you feel about taking a course in computing—to include word-processing?'

This was wonderful! Lissa could no longer try to put on a show of cool dignity. She smiled widely and the dimple appeared in her left cheek. 'Oh, *yes*, I'd love it, it's what I've wanted for ages.'

Dark brows rose warningly. 'Hold on a minute. Don't get too enthusiastic until you hear what I have in mind. I'm working on finalising details for the launching of a new micro in the autumn. If you agree, you can help me with it.'

'Help? I couldn't possibly. I don't know anything about computers. I told you——'

He lifted a hand to cut off her protest. Then he smiled.

It was the first time he had smiled at her and it had a most curious effect. She found herself staring at his face—at the crinkles beside the eyes which were that unusual shade of light grey, at the thick, silky lashes, at the thin, sculptured lips and the flash of white teeth against bronzed skin. Suddenly she felt dizzy and the room began to revolve in front of her eyes. She blinked hard and it stopped revolving. How strange! She must be weaker than she thought.

'What a girl you are for jumping the gun,' he was saying tolerantly. 'I realise you don't know anything about computers—that's exactly why I want you. What I need is a guinea-pig.'

'Oh, yes?' she said idiotically. She seemed to have lost completely the thread of the conversation. He went on talking—vaguely she knew it was something about a manual he was writing for the new computer. 'A good idea, don't you think?'

Lissa looked into the grey eyes that were searching her own, waiting for her reply. His eyes seemed to change colour—now they were not steely but silvery. 'Hm?' she breathed vaguely. 'Oh—oh, yes.' She hadn't a very clear idea of what she was agreeing to. Her brain wasn't working properly and everything seemed fuzzy at the moment.

'Splendid. You've got your passport with you?'

Passport. Why would she need a passport? She closed her eyes and tried to concentrate. Then she remembered putting all her personal papers in a wallet in her case before locking her desk at home, so it must still be there. 'Yes,' she said.

'Good,' he said briskly, and stood up. 'It will all work out splendidly, you'll see. We'll be killing four birds with one stone, to coin a phrase. I'll see you tomorrow—look after yourself, little guinea-pig.' He leaned over and ran a finger down her cheek briefly.

Then he was gone and the room was suddenly empty and silent. Birds! Guinea-pig! What did all that mean? She wished she could remember clearly what he'd been talking about. The world had suddenly turned into an unfamiliar place where anything might happen next.

What happened next was that the cheery little maid came in with her lunch tray. She fussed round, arranging it on a lap-table, and said, 'Your favourite poached salmon and fresh garden peas, Miss Stephens. My, aren't you looking better, then? A real nice colour you've got in your cheeks. And isn't your hair lovely—ooh, I'd give anything for hair like yours.' She stood admiring the froth of shining chestnut curls round Lissa's small face, until she suddenly remembered all the other trays waiting for her to deliver, and hurried away.

After lunch Lissa's nurse came in to settle her down for her afternoon sleep.

Lissa put a hand on her forehead. 'Nurse—did I—did the doctor say anything about my having slight concussion? I felt sort of light-headed just now and I wondered...'

The nurse shook her head reassuringly. 'No concussion. They tested for that when you came in. You're still a little weak, that's all it is. Now you lie down and have a nice sleep, my dear.'

Lissa lay down obediently but sleep was far away. 'Oh, *damn*,' she said aloud. This was ridiculous. What had happened to make her almost black out for a few seconds? And why couldn't she remember exactly what Hugh Winchester had said? It must be merely a temporary aberration. Tomorrow it would have gone away and she would recall the whole conversation. Oh, well, she must put it out of her mind—treat it like a name she'd forgotten, which would suddenly come back when she was thinking about something else. She sat up and reached for the detective novel she was reading.

It was quite a while before she realised that she was holding the book upside-down.

Next morning Lissa woke up feeling much better. She still couldn't recall the whole of that interview with Hugh Winchester yesterday. She did remember something about a passport and she had a hazy idea that she might have agreed to go somewhere with him. *That* was out for a start. She found him overpowering and slightly alarming and she certainly wasn't going anywhere with him; she was going to Cornwall to spend the next few days with her cousin Jean. He couldn't refuse to give her sick-leave, could he?

She tried several times to get Jean on the phone, without success. Oh, well, she would just have to turn up at the hotel. There would be someone there—Jean wouldn't shut the place up in April, when bookings would be expected.

Matron came in as she was brushing her hair and putting on a touch of lipstick, which was all the make-up she would need for a train trip to Cornwall.

'Good morning, Miss Stephens. Getting ready for the big world outside?' She was a friendly middle-aged woman, tall and composed and extremely professional. 'How are you feeling?'

'Oh, fine, thank you,' Lissa said. 'How could I not after all the care you've taken of me?' She hesitated. 'I should so have liked to show my gratitude to the nurses and the little maid who waited on me, but I'm afraid it was all so sudden and I haven't got . . .'

The matron held up a hand, smiling. 'Don't worry, that's all been taken care of by Mr Winchester. He's here, by the way, waiting for you. Nurse will take you along to the lounge and bring your travelling case and your coat to you.' She held out a hand. 'The best of luck, Miss Stephens, and thank you for being such a model patient.' With a swish of her stylishly pleated maroon skirt she passed on to the next patient.

He's here, waiting for you. Lissa's stomach felt hollow. Why did the man have such a devastating effect on her?

Her day-nurse came in. 'All ready, Miss Stephens?' She smiled. 'Shall I help you on with your coat? And Matron says you can take the walking-stick with you. It will probably be a help.'

Lissa pulled herself to her feet and fumbled her way into her light coat. She gripped the handle of the walking-stick as if it were a venomous snake. The nurse took her other arm, picked up the travelling bag in her free hand and together they proceeded to the lift.

'Here she is, all safe and sound, Mr Winchester.' The nurse's smile was noticeably arch as she led Lissa into the room where Hugh Winchester was standing looking out of the window.

He turned immediately and took Lissa's travelling case. 'Thank you, Nurse, I'll look after Miss Stephens now. I expect you're busy. And we're very grateful for your excellent care and attention, aren't we, Lissa?'

'Yes—oh, yes, thank you, Nurse,' Lissa mumbled, not looking at him. 'Everyone's been marvellous.'

'All part of the job.' The nurse smiled with un-accustomed flippancy, her gaze switching immediately to Hugh. 'Have a safe trip,' she added. And with another beaming smile she whisked away.

Hugh stood quite still, gazing down at Lissa. 'You're looking better,' he said. His eyes were silvery this morning, reflecting the sunlight coming through the window.

Keep cool, she told herself, cool and business-like. Which was made more difficult by the fact that he didn't look at all businesslike himself today, in a lightweight suit and a thin striped shirt. 'I'm quite better, thank you, Mr Winchester. I'm most grateful to you for arranging all this for me. I've decided to go straight to Cornwall, to my cousin's, so if you wouldn't mind taking me to Paddington...'

He smiled blandly. 'I should mind very much,' he said. 'I have a taxi waiting outside to take us to Heathrow. I have also booked a flight for you to Paris. So I'm afraid your cousin is going to be dis-appointed. No doubt you can phone her later and explain.'

Lissa blinked. 'I really don't know what you're talking about, Mr Winchester. I certainly didn't agree to go to Paris with you.'

'You certainly did,' he told her firmly. 'Come along, we mustn't keep the taxi waiting. Bring that walking-stick, it's a good idea.' He picked up her case, linked an arm firmly with hers and led her out to the taxi. Short of struggling, there was nothing Lissa could do but go with him, and the strong grip of his hand on her arm was making her feel helpless. Helpless, and shaky inside.

In the taxi she sat as far into a corner as she could and drew in a deep breath. 'I don't think I was properly awake when you came to see me yesterday and I must have got things mixed up. I really don't know anything about going to Paris with you, and if I did agree, then I've changed my mind. I hope it won't inconvenience you,' she added politely, remembering that her job was probably on the line and she mustn't antagonise him.

'Oh, dear,' he said, with an edge of amusement to his voice. 'Do I have to go through it all again? Briefly, I suggested that you should solve your homelessness problem by accompanying me to Paris, where I'll be working on preparing the manual for the new computer that's being launched in the autumn. As you told me you know nothing about computing, I thought you'd be a very useful guinea-pig to try it out on. That seemed the logical way out of the difficulty, and you appeared to be very keen on the idea.'

'Did I?' Lissa said faintly.

'You certainly did. Thus encouraged, I went ahead and made the arrangements—booked our afternoon flight today and so on.'

The deep, composed voice was having an odd, tranquillising effect on Lissa. But to go to Paris with Hugh Winchester! To work closely with him, see him every day! She didn't know whether she could stand up to that. He was so—so—overwhelming.

She played a final, desperate card. She met his eyes across the width of the cab and forced a tight smile to her mouth. 'And how would I know, Mr

Winchester, that I'd be any safer going to Paris with
you than going to Scotland with Paul?'

He actually laughed, the brute. 'You'd have to
take my word for your personal safety, little girl.
But I assure you I don't go in for cradle-snatching.'

He must have seen her eyes blaze into green fire,
and perhaps regretted his words, for he went on
more gently, 'And as a final reassurance I may
add—as you don't seem to have taken in all I said
the other day—we shall be staying at my mother's
home, just outside Paris.' After a pause, in which
Lissa was completely unable to say a word, he
added, 'Well? Are you satisfied?'

Her mouth was dry as sawdust. 'I—I suppose
so,' she muttered.

'Good,' he said suavely. 'I thought I could persuade you.'

Lissa closed her eyes and leaned her head back.
There was an almost hypnotic quality about this
man that made him difficult to oppose. She would
have to fight her vulnerability where Hugh
Winchester was concerned or goodness knew where
it would lead her. Lead her? What was she thinking
of? It wasn't going to lead her anywhere.

Their relationship would be on a strictly business
basis and she stood to gain from it, she reminded
herself. He had promised that she would learn the
technology she so much wanted to learn.

All he required of her in return was to be a
guinea-pig. She must remind herself of that when
her common sense threatened to desert her.

CHAPTER THREE

AT HEATHROW Hugh insisted on securing a wheel-chair for Lissa, and trundled her around without the slightest sign of embarrassment.

The embarrassment was all hers. 'I'm sure I can walk,' she said, craning her neck round to frown up at him.

'Of course you can,' he told her and went on pushing imperturbably, 'but not just yet.'

Lissa sighed and submitted. When she was quite fit again, she promised herself, she would have to show this high-handed individual that she wasn't going to take orders from him so meekly.

But she had to admit that there was still slight uneasiness—not exactly pain—in her knee when she moved around, especially climbing steps, and she was relieved to sink into the luxury of a seat in the plane's first-class compartment.

'Comfortable?' Hugh enquired formally, when they were airborne.

'Very,' Lissa said a little shortly. 'I've been very comfortable for the last six days—at your expense, Mr Winchester. And I'm certainly not used to first-class air travel. It's probably very ungrateful of me, but actually I feel as if I'm being——' she swallowed '—being patronised.'

She caught a gleam of amusement in the clear silvery grey eyes. 'Not patronised, Lissa, I assure you. I'm merely taking the best care of my little guinea-pig. As I would do with any other small, wounded animal, I hope.'

'Oh, now you're making fun of me. You're— you're impossible.' She turned her head away from him and her shining curls bounced into her neck.

She heard his laugh and bit her lip with annoyance, staring down at the coast of England, fast disappearing below.

'Drink, Lissa? Or would you prefer tea?'

She looked round to find a smiling stewardess standing beside them. 'Oh, tea, please,' she said eagerly.

Rather to her surprise he told the girl, 'We'll both have tea, and anything nice you can offer to eat.' She had expected Hugh Winchester to order something more sophisticated than tea.

When the stewardess had gone he said, 'I always have afternoon tea when available. I think it's one of the more civilised customs still left to us. I take it you agree?' As Lissa nodded he added drily, 'That's one thing we have in common then. We'll have to see if we can't find some more, won't we?'

He didn't wait for her to reply. He went on, 'Now, I'd better put you in the picture about the set-up at my mother's home. It's a largish house not very far from Paris. My mother is French and after her divorce from my father she married a Frenchman called Claude Delage. He's in the art world and spends a great deal of time at his gallery in Paris. I have my own rooms in the house so that I can work there now and again and see something of my mother.' He turned his head to look down out of the window at the flat fields below. 'She's not been too well lately—I've been a bit worried about her.'

Lissa said quickly, 'Oh, then surely she won't want to have visitors. I don't think you should have brought me.'

He shook his head. 'She'll enjoy meeting someone new, she always does. And there's an excellent housekeeper, Marie, who has been with her for some time. Also a young maid. No, Lissa, you won't be any bother, I assure you.'

Tea arrived then, with an assortment of little cream biscuits. After Lissa had poured out, Hugh bit into a biscuit and said, 'Any questions?'

Lissa thought for a time and then ventured, 'The company—it belongs to you? I just wondered...'

His face hardened. He said stiffly, 'As you're so interested, Paul inherited a sizeable part of the company on my father's death, due, no doubt, to the urging of my stepmother. He also draws a sizeable slice of the profits. Paul is no blood relation of mine, thank heaven.'

Lissa gave him a straight look. 'I'm not in the least interested in Paul's income,' she said frostily.

'No? Well, if I've misjudged the situation, I'm sorry. But you see, I'm all too familiar with my stepbrother's charming little ways, and I take great exception to his using office hours to pursue his—er—amorous adventures.'

Lissa said slowly, 'You really hate him, don't you?'

'Yes,' he said simply.

There was a silence. She guessed that there was a great deal more he could have said. But it was clear that he wasn't going to say it.

'And you believe me when I say there was nothing between Paul and me?'

'I find it difficult to believe. If you've got some silly notion of supporting Paul's cause I'm afraid you're on a loser. I can't credit that Paul would leave a girl like you alone for very long. You're a very lovely little guinea-pig, Lissa.' Lightly he touched a curl that was resting against her cheek.

She tossed her head away from him. 'And that's another thing,' she said tartly. 'I think the guinea-pig thing has worn rather thin, don't you? I've agreed to help you with your manual. I've told you I haven't been trained in computer work. But that doesn't mean that I'm some dim little nitwit and I must say I resent being treated as one.'

'Sorry,' he said, but he didn't sound sorry, he sounded amused. 'In future I'll try not to be so annoying, if you'll try not to be so prickly.'

'I'm not . . .' she began.

She saw the smile reach his eyes and after a moment felt her lips twitch.

'That's better,' he said comfortably. 'And I *don't* think you're a dim little nitwit. If I did I should never have suggested trying you on this project.'

'Well—thank you. After those kind words I just hope I'll be able to take it all in. I wasn't awfully good at maths at school.'

Hugh grinned encouragingly. 'You don't have to have a mathematical brain,' he said. 'Just ordinary common sense is needed for what I'm asking of you. If you want to go further with computing— to learn programming, for instance—then you do need a rather special kind of brain—the kind that can approach problems in a detailed, logical manner. But let's take it one step at a time, shall we?' He pushed his cup along the table. 'Now, may I have another cup of tea, please?'

It was still light when the taxi from Charles de Gaulle Airport stopped in the drive of a tall, graceful old house, surrounded by its own gardens, in a tree-lined road on the outskirts of Paris.

Hugh's mother opened the front door to them herself. Lissa had a first impression of a tall, rather frail figure in a clinging pastel-blue gown. Her hair was black, except for silvery wings over each ear, and taken back into a knot on top of her head. Very bright brown eyes glistened as she hugged her son. Lissa guessed that she had been waiting with excitement for the sound of the taxi.

'How are you, Maman?' Hugh kissed her on both cheeks and held her away, searching her face. 'You look better.'

'Oh, I *am* better; my new doctor's such a sweetie, he's taking such good care of me.'

Holding Hugh's hand, she turned immediately to Lissa. 'And this is Lissa?' Her English was perfect, with only the very faintest accent. She held out her other hand in the friendliest manner and Lissa didn't miss the quick, interested look that assessed her from head to foot. 'Hugh told me about your nasty accident—what a horrid thing to happen. Come along in and rest and we'll have a drink before dinner.' She looked back to her son. 'Help Lissa into the drawing-room, *chéri*. She must be tired.'

'I can manage, thanks,' Lissa said hastily. She stooped and picked up her walking-stick, which

Hugh had deposited with her travelling bag outside the door. She had an idea that he intended to pick her up and carry her bodily into the house, and she felt a tingle run all through her body at the thought.

He smiled ruefully at his mother. 'Lissa is an independent young woman, Maman. You have to be very firm to get her to accept help.'

'Don't believe him, Madame Delage. Mr Winchester has been very kind and arranged for me to be looked after splendidly since my fall.' Lissa followed her hostess into a long room where a cheerful fire burned in a grate with a richly decorated marble overmantel. She had a quick impression of elegance and comfort cleverly combined in the beautiful pieces of period furniture, the Chinese rugs on the polished parquet floor, contrasting with the modern sofas and lounge chairs and the contemporary paintings on the walls.

'Bring Lissa to the fire, Hugh, the evening is going to be quite chilly,' his mother said, and added to Lissa, 'In Paris everyone has a nasty habit of turning the heat off on the first of April, but my years in England have made me more flexible, and I do so love an open fire.'

Hugh pulled out a small gilt chair for Lissa, saying that she would be more comfortable in a straight-backed chair than in one of the deep loungers. He drew up a low marquetry table beside her and brought a crystal glass half filled with what she guessed was brandy and water.

'Just what you need after the journey,' he said, placing an encouraging hand on her shoulder.

He was being altogether too attentive, Lissa thought. She caught his mother's eyes upon them when Hugh leaned over to straighten the cushion behind Lissa's back. He hadn't treated her like this in London. What was the idea?

She sipped her brandy and listened to Hugh and his mother exchanging small talk about their journey, about a forthcoming exhibition at the Delage gallery, and finally about the weather, which apparently had been particularly good lately.

Madame Delage turned to Lissa. 'April in Paris! You will be too young, Lissa, to remember that romantic old song. But Paris is truly romantic in April. You have been to Paris before?'

Lissa shook her head. 'I've been to France twice with school parties, but never to Paris.'

'Then you will see it at its best while you are here. Hugh will show you all the exciting places, will you not, *chéri*? The Louvre and Montmartre and Notre Dame—and the river, of course and...'

Hugh held up a hand, laughing. 'Steady on, Maman. Don't forget I've brought Lissa here to help me with my work. We're going to be busy.'

'But not too busy,' his mother insisted. 'And if you're going to be an old workaholic I shall find some nice young man to show Lissa the sights.'

He sighed heavily. 'Take care, Lissa, my mother is an incurable romantic.'

Madame Delage laughed and pulled a face at him as she got up from her chair. 'Of course I am, love is what makes the world go round, hadn't you heard? Now come along, Lissa, if you've finished your drink I'll take you to your room. You can have a good rest before dinner.'

Lissa stood too, and began to follow her hostess, but at the door Madame Delage stopped and turned back. 'We've put Lissa in your room, Hugh dear, as it's on the ground floor, and you can have the room next to the linen cupboard upstairs. Marie has moved your things. I'm sure you won't mind. I didn't want Lissa to have to struggle with the stairs—I remember how painful getting up and down stairs was when I broke my ankle that time.'

If Hugh made any comment she didn't wait for it, but linked her arm with Lissa's and took her across the wide, marble-floored hall, down a passage, through a door and into a vast bedroom, switching on lights as she went.

'A very masculine room, I'm afraid.' Madame Delage moved round, straightening a lace mat on the solid mahogany chest, pulling a faded leaf from a vase of pink roses on the dressing-table. 'Marie— my housekeeper—has tried to pretty it up a little, as you see. But at least the bed is most comfortable.' She bounced up and down cheerfully on the quilted damask bedspread that covered the large double bed.

'I'll send Hugh in with your case,' she said, 'and then you must lie down and have a rest. You'll have plenty of time to take a shower, if you care to, before dinner at eight o'clock. The shower-room is through that door, and the other door communicates with Hugh's office—where I suppose you'll be working with him.'

Lissa stood hesitantly in the middle of the big room, feeling rather overawed. 'I haven't brought anything at all "special" to wear for dinner, *madame*,' she said. 'It was all decided rather— rather suddenly, about my coming.' How much had Hugh told his mother about the circumstances of his unexpected decision to bring her with him? she wondered.

'Don't worry a bit. You look very pretty as you are. Navy and white is always so smart and becoming. And please—Monique, not *"Madame"*. I lived in England so long that I got used to the way Christian names are used all the time. It seems so much friendlier. Now you must wear exactly what you like.' She touched Lissa's arm almost shyly. 'I'm so glad Hugh brought you, my dear,' she said. 'So very, *very* glad.'

She went swiftly out of the room before Lissa had had time to wonder what, if anything, was meant by that rather odd remark.

Hugh arrived with her case a couple of minutes later. He put it down on a chair beside the bed and stood looking around, his expression inscrutable. He had taken off his tie and unfastened the top button of his shirt to disclose his neck, smooth and faintly suntanned. Lissa found her eyes fixed on the taut muscles of his throat, until she realised what she was doing and looked away quickly.

She walked across to the dressing-table and rested her hand on the polished surface. 'Are you cross about being pushed out of your room? I'm so sorry,' she said over her shoulder. 'Your mother's very kind and thoughtful, but I'm sure I could have managed the stairs.'

'No, she's quite right—you'll be more comfortable here. I was just thinking...'

She waited, tilting her head, watching his face in the mirror.

'I was just thinking,' Hugh Winchester said softly, 'how pleasant it would be if we could share it.'

'Oh!' gasped Lisa, utterly taken aback.

His lips twitched. 'That remark puts me in brother Paul's league, so I won't make it, I'll just think it.' He walked to the door. 'See you at dinner,' he said, and went out.

Feeling a delicate warmth spread over her, Lissa sank on to the dressing-stool. 'Well!' she gasped.

Of course that remark wasn't meant to be taken seriously. Most men thought it rather dashing to trot out suggestive remarks to girls. But she wouldn't have thought Hugh Winchester needed to parade his sexy charisma. She would simply forget all about that remark, it didn't mean a thing.

Which made it all the more annoying that, as she turned back the duvet and sank down into the soft bed, she should keep on remembering it, and remembering the provocative gleam in his silvery grey eyes...

She wished Monique hadn't found it necessary to give her Hugh's bedroom. The bed-linen was freshly laundered and smelled delicately of stephanotis—a perfume which she could hardly imagine Hugh using!—but all the same there was something far too intimate about lying here and remembering his words—meant as a joke, of course.

Impatiently, she swung her legs off the bed. She would unpack her case and take a shower. Mooning over Hugh Winchester was not what she had come here for. She had come here as an employee of the company; she had come to work.

She slid back the heavy door of the wardrobe. It was empty except for an evening suit at the end of the rail, which must be Hugh's. Lissa touched the fine midnight-blue material delicately. He would look quite gorgeous in evening dress.

She snatched her hand away as if it had been burned. This wouldn't do at all, she was in danger of getting an adolescent crush on the man. Hastily she began to unpack her case, hanging her own clothes as far as possible from the suit that was already there.

When she had finished she regarded the result doubtfully. Packing for what she had supposed was going to be a business trip with Paul, she had included mostly plain, smart, tailored outfits—the navy suit she was wearing, a lighter cream one in case the weather turned warm. Several blouses, white and cream and patterned. There were two dresses, to wear if they went out for a meal in the evening, and that was all. She selected one of the two dresses—a pretty little amber number in blessedly creaseless Terylene with short sleeves and a demure neckline—laid it out on the bed, and went to have a shower.

She was putting the finishing touches to her make-up when there was a tap on the door and Monique came into the room, wearing a simple black dress of which every stitch proclaimed Paris.

'Dinner's nearly ready,' she said. 'I came to show you the way to the dining-room. This house is a little baffling at first.'

As Lissa got quickly to her feet Monique went on, 'My dear, you look charming. That colour almost matches your hair. And I love the embroidery round the neck.' She sighed. 'I've reached the age when the only choice is between black and pastels. Claude—that's my husband—says I should go in for vivid colours, but somehow I don't feel right in them.'

Lissa liked Hugh's mother, felt at ease with her. She said, 'Oh, I love black, it's so wonderfully sophisticated. It suits you so well.' She grinned ruefully. 'But my self-confidence isn't up to wearing the "little black dress".'

Monique laughed. 'We must go shopping while you're here, Lissa. You shall buy a little black dress and I will buy a daring scarlet one, and we'll come back brimming over with confidence, both of us, how about that?'

Lissa joined in the laughter. 'I'm afraid my budget won't run to shopping in Paris, but I'd love to come and watch you choose. That is, if I'm allowed time off by your son.'

'Oh, pooh to that—I shall arrange it.' There was more than a hint of authority in the statement. Was this where Hugh inherited his high-handed ways from? Lissa wondered who would win, in a fight. Hugh's mother might look frail but she would be someone to be reckoned with.

'You must certainly have time off,' Monique went on. 'He must take you out and about, as I told him. It will do him good—he works far too hard.'

'Oh, but he brought me here to help him with the manual he's writing,' Lissa said hastily. 'He won't want to entertain me.'

'Won't he?' The dark eyes were quizzical. 'We'll see. Well, if you're ready, Lissa, shall we go along to the salon, where I'm sure my husband will be dispensing drinks.'

In the salon Hugh was standing with his back to the window and beside him was a stunningly attractive girl with sleek silver-gilt hair, wearing a peacock-blue outfit that lit up the amazing blue of her eyes.

She ran across to Monique and kissed her on both cheeks. 'So sweet of you to have me, *madame*. I'm afraid I invited myself when I heard that Hugh was expected. It's such ages since I saw him.'

Beside her, Hugh smiled tolerantly. 'Six weeks,' he said.

'It feels like six centuries.' She had a slight lisp. 'He's my guardian angel—I simply can't get along without him, you know.' She laughed prettily.

Monique smiled a little wryly. 'Yes, I know that, Carolyn.' She put a hand at Lissa's arm and drew her forward. 'Lissa, this is Carolyn Blake, who helps my husband at the gallery. Carolyn, Lissa Stephens, a friend of Hugh's from England.'

The girl froze and the pretty colour drained out of her cheeks. Lissa might have said, You needn't worry, I'm only a girl who's working for Hugh, a little guinea-pig he rescued from his randy stepbrother. Instead, she held out a hand, smiling politely. 'Hello,' she said.

Carolyn touched her hand as if it were a wet rag and turned back to Hugh, who had been standing watching the three women, an unreadable expression on his handsome face.

'Hughie—I've got such a lot to tell you. I'm really enjoying working at the gallery and my French is improving and Claude says he is pleased with me.'

She linked her arm with Hugh's and smiled winningly up at him. 'It was marvellous of you to get me the job—but then, you're always so good to me.'

'Oh, I *am* good,' he said, dead-pan.

Lissa watched the little scene and felt her eyebrows lifting. Didn't Hugh realise that the girl was putting on an act? Or—wasn't it an act at all, but rather the intimate, playful exchange of two people very close to one another? And why was that idea so distasteful to her?

Monique's hand was on her arm. 'Come and meet my husband, Lissa.' She led Lissa across the long room to where a tall, thin man was concentrating upon a variety of bottles set out on a table whose dark, polished wood gleamed almost as brilliantly as the array of crystal glasses upon it.

When they had been introduced Claude Delage took Lissa's hand and kissed it with a little flourish. '*Enchanté, mademoiselle.* We must all assure ourselves that you enjoy your stay with us.'

'Thank you,' Lissa said. She wished that Hugh had made it plain to his parents that she was merely an employee of the firm, here to work for him. It was embarrassing to be greeted as if she were an honoured and important guest. But she guessed that Claude Delage would have been equally gallant even if he had been forewarned of her lowly status.

She watched him while he poured out drinks for her and for his wife—Lissa had asked rather shyly for white wine and been reassured by his evident approval of her choice. She decided that the word for him was elegant. Elegant, sophisticated, a touch cynical, perhaps. And very handsome. The look that passed between him and his wife as he handed her a glass told her that they were very much in love.

Carolyn had drawn Hugh over to a sofa beside the fireplace and was talking animatedly to him, one white hand resting on his knee. Monique glanced at them and raised well-shaped eyebrows towards her husband. 'I, too, am entitled to a little of my son's company, don't you think?' She swished across the room towards them, and Hugh immediately stood up and joined his mother, throwing an arm affectionately round her shoulders, leaving Carolyn sitting alone, with a pout on her pretty mouth.

Lissa heard Claude Delage's little chuckle. Then he turned back to her courteously. 'You are quite recovered from your accident, Mademoiselle Stephens?'

'Yes, thank you. And please call me Lissa, won't you?'

'*Certainement.*' The clever dark eyes surveyed her with interest. 'You have known Hugh for a long time, yes?'

'Oh, no,' she said hastily. 'Only a few days.' She must make her position clear straight away. But before she could think of the words, Claude Delage, to her astonishment, leaned forward and kissed her on both cheeks.

'Ah, *un coup de foudre*,' he murmured. 'That is excellent.'

Coup de foudre—what did that mean? Lissa's O-level French reminded her that *coup* was a blow or a knock. Was he talking about her fall down the stairs? She smiled vaguely and sipped her wine. She liked the tall Frenchman, she liked Monique, she liked—yes, *liked* Hugh. Nothing more.

Carolyn she disliked on sight. It surprised her a little, for she wasn't in the habit of taking a violent dislike to strangers. But the way the girl had been hanging on to Hugh's arm and yearning up into his eyes had been—had been *disgusting*. She hoped Carolyn wasn't going to be around much while she was here.

She was certainly making the most of her time while she *was* here. She kept close to Hugh's side when they all went into the dining-room. While Monique was engaged at the back of the room with a small woman in a black dress—presumably Marie the housekeeper—Carolyn managed to slip into the chair next to Hugh's, leaning towards him as he filled her wine glass—*ogling* him, Lissa thought. She really was absurdly, embarrassingly obvious.

The dinner was superbly cooked but Lissa's appetite seemed to have deserted her. She sat on Monsieur Delage's right at the long, elegantly appointed table and toyed with her duck and tiny green peas served with a wonderfully subtle sauce, and the lemon sorbet that followed.

'Marie hasn't lost any of her culinary art,' Hugh observed.

Sitting next to him, Carolyn sighed and murmured, *'Elle est une chef tout-à-fait merveilleuse.'*

Hugh bestowed a quizzical look on her. 'Your accent is improving, darling,' he said. 'But I think it should be *un*, not *une*. Am I right, Claude?'

Claude Delage's face wrinkled into a smile. 'Ah, yes, the chef is still masculine. We have not yet come to terms with feminism in our cuisine.'

Everyone laughed dutifully, but Lissa thought that Carolyn's laughter was somewhat forced. And when Hugh added, 'But we shall speak English while Lissa is among us,' she pouted mutinously.

'Unless,' Hugh went on, 'you're acquainted with our lingo, Lissa?'

'Only as far as O-level.'

She wanted to add, But please don't let that put you out, especially when *darling* Carolyn is getting on so well. After all, I'm only a mere guinea-pig. But even letting herself think it would count as being 'prickly', wouldn't it? Something Hugh had warned her against.

So, instead, she leaned towards Monique and said quietly, 'Would it be terribly rude of me to go to my room? I feel rather tired, suddenly.'

'My dear, of course you must. I shall come with you.' Her hostess stood up and took Lissa's hand. 'This poor child has overdone things a little,' she announced. 'I'm going to insist on her going straight to bed. Come along, Lissa.'

With a murmured apology and without looking at anyone in particular, Lissa obeyed. She was aware that Hugh had half risen from his chair and then sat down again. He was no doubt heartily relieved to have the responsibility of her transferred to his mother.

Ten minutes later Lissa was ensconced in the big double bed—Hugh's bed, only she didn't want to think about that. Monique had been kind, and concerned that Lissa had everything she needed, and had gone back to the dining-room with a promise that Katrine, the maid, would bring a warm drink.

'And I'll bring you some tablets when dinner is over—just in case you can't sleep. You aren't in pain, are you?'

Lissa shook her head. 'Oh, no—just tired.'

She felt a fraud, because she could easily have stayed up—as far as her physical condition was concerned. But her feelings were another matter. And she had felt very strongly that she couldn't stay another moment at the dinner table.

What was the matter with her? She'd always rather prided herself on her common sense. Perhaps the doctors had been wrong. Perhaps she was suffering from the bump on her head when she'd fallen down the stairs. She remembered how she had partially blacked out when Hugh had been talking to her in the nursing home.

She was beginning to feel angry that she had submitted so tamely to Hugh's insistence on bringing her to France with him. In spite of the warm welcome she had received from his mother and his stepfather—or perhaps because of it—she felt ill at ease and vaguely embarrassed. And the trouble was she didn't know why.

The little maid, Katrine, brought her a milky drink and she sipped it slowly and wished she had a book to read—she always liked to read for a while in bed. She must ask Monique for one tomorrow. She lay back against the cool, delicately scented pillow and tried to sort out her feelings.

Common sense told her there wasn't anything to sort out. She'd come here to do a job for Hugh Winchester, that was all, and it was no concern of hers if he was being blatantly pursued by a girl with silver-gilt hair and baby-blue eyes. That was his

problem—and she didn't suppose it was a problem
at all because men liked being flattered, didn't they?
She had never been much good at flattery herself
and it made her wince inwardly to witness the act
that some girls put on.

There was a light tap on the door and she called
out, 'Come in, *madame*.'

The door opened and it was Hugh who came into
the room. Lissa's throat went dry suddenly and she
pulled the duvet a little higher. To pull it up to her
chin would seem ridiculously prim, but she was
hotly aware that her nightdress, with its narrow
crêpe de Chine shoulder-straps, was embarrassingly revealing.

He came across the room to the bed, one hand
held out towards her. For a dazed moment she
thought he meant to reach out—to touch her—and
her heart gave a great throb and began to beat
suffocatingly.

But he was merely offering her a strip of tablets
in their plastic cover. 'My mother asked me to bring
these to you,' he said with a faint smile, and it was
obvious that he had noted her alarm. 'I had to come
along to rescue my shaving gear. The only thing
that Marie overlooked when she was doing her re-
moving act. May I, please?'

'Of course,' said Lissa and it came out like a
croak. 'Help yourself.'

He disappeared into the shower-room and
emerged a moment later carrying a razor-case, a fat
tube and a bottle of lotion.

He stood at the foot of the bed, regarding her,
still with that faint smile touching his mouth. 'You
look very comfy, Lissa. Are you feeling better?'

His eyes went with obvious pleasure to the creamy skin of her arms and neck, lingering on the soft swell of her breasts, only partially hidden by her nightdress.

She swallowed. 'I'm fine, thanks, just a bit tired. I'll be ready to start work whenever you need me, Mr Winchester.'

'Oh, no hurry. Find your way around first. My mother's delighted to have you here. She wants to take you into Paris to the shops, she tells me. You must make the most of your stay, Lissa. You might even like to touch up your French while you have the opportunity. And I'd like it if you'd drop the "Mr Winchester" while we're here. The name's Hugh.' He wandered off towards the door.

Lissa said, 'Talking of French...'

He turned round. 'Yes?'

'I just wondered—what does *coup de foudre* mean?'

Hugh's dark brows rose. 'It means thunder-bolt—lightning strike—anything of that sort.' The grey eyes met hers, narrowing wickedly. 'It's also a term used for that mythical illness called love at first sight. You can take your pick, young Lissa.' The smile disappeared and he looked hard at her across the room. 'Why?' he said. 'Why do you want to know?'

As usual, Lissa found it impossible to hold that probing gaze. She fixed her eyes on the pattern of the duvet cover. 'Oh, it's nothing important. Just something I came across—in a book,' she added, for good measure.

'I see,' he said slowly. 'Well, goodnight, Lissa.'

He went out and Lissa was left staring at the panelled wood of the door which had closed behind him. For minutes she sat motionless, her eyes wide, shocked. *Love at first sight.*

No, it couldn't be.

Could it?

Hugh walking into the office, dark and fabulously handsome and livid with anger because Paul was kissing her. Hugh sitting beside her on the stairs after she had fallen. Hugh lifting her in his arms to carry her out to his car...

Memory took her back as far as that. Then her mind wasn't working at all. Only her body was functioning and her body was giving her all sorts of unfamiliar, disturbing messages.

She was unaware of time passing. At last she sank down into the softness of the big bed—Hugh's bed. *Love at first sight.* One hand went out and switched off the bedside light. Her eyes closed softly and her arms wrapped themselves round her breast. She sighed luxuriously.

'Yes,' she murmured into the pillow. 'Oh, yes.'

CHAPTER FOUR

IN THE clear light of the next morning common sense returned. As Lissa sat up in bed and enjoyed the breakfast of croissants, preserves and strong coffee brought to her by Katrine, the little maid, she argued the situation out with herself.

If she wanted to learn computing—which she did—she would need to use logic. Lissa wasn't too sure that she had the right kind of brain. But one thing that stared her in the face was that she certainly wasn't being logical about falling in love with Hugh Winchester.

Try to set out the situation logically, Lissa, it will be good practice, she thought. She munched a hunk of croissant dabbed with apricot preserve and thought hard. Then she took a notebook from her handbag and wrote neatly:

> *Fact:* It is just plain silly to imagine you're in love with a man you've only known for about a week, and only seen three or four times.
>
> *Question:* Would you really be feeble enough to fall in love with a man who treated you like a not-too-bright fourth-former?
>
> *Question:* Have you forgotten that the only reason he brought you here was because A, you might be useful to him and B, he wanted to make sure you wouldn't hold

the company responsible for your accident?

Fact: You certainly couldn't hope to compete with the disgustingly sexy Carolyn.

Fact: Hugh Winchester is a powerfully attractive man. No denying that. Last night you had merely been reacting to his physical magnetism. All the rest was fantasy. The fantasy has been lovely while it lasted but you can't live in a world of fantasy.

Conclusion: You are not, repeat not, in love with Hugh Winchester.

There, how was that for a logical run-down of the situation? Maybe she did have a logical mind after all.

She snapped the notebook shut, tossed down a final cup of coffee and got briskly out of bed to shower, noticing with satisfaction that this morning her knee felt perfectly normal again for the first time.

She dressed in her businesslike navy skirt and white blouse, applied make-up sparingly, brushed her shining mop of chestnut curls and opened the door that communicated with Hugh's office.

There was nobody there. She stood in the middle of the room, taking it all in. It was a smaller room than the bedroom next door, but equally neat and orderly. In a way it resembled a corner of the office back in London, with computers on work-stations, a photocopier, a shredding machine, and a small desk near the window. Venetian blinds were pulled down and the morning sun threw bars of light across the desk, with its tidy piles of notebooks and folders. Beside the desk was a large bin full to the top with shredded computer print-outs. Of course, Hugh wouldn't want this new work to lie about for anyone to read.

The door into the corridor opened and Lissa spun round. Monique stood there, smiling, wearing a cream pleated skirt and a tailored linen blouse. 'I thought I might find you here, Lissa. Did you sleep well?'

'Marvellously, thank you. I'm completely better now and ready for work.'

Monique looked round the tidy office and shrugged helplessly. 'I haven't a clue what goes on here and I'm afraid Hugh isn't here to put you in the picture.' She stooped to brush an invisible speck from her skirt. 'He drove Carolyn back to Paris after dinner—he keeps a car of his own here. He rang later to say he had an appointment in Paris this morning so he wouldn't bother to drive back here again last night. Claude has a bed in his office at the gallery.' She hesitated, a little frown settling between her intelligent brown eyes. 'I expect Hugh intended to sleep there.'

But you don't believe he did sleep there, Lissa thought, and you don't like what that means. Oh, and neither do I, a voice wailed inside her. The sudden picture of Hugh in bed with Carolyn, of her pale gold hair spilling over the pillow, of her mouth raised seductively to his, of his hands on her soft limbs, filled Lissa with seething, impotent misery.

It wouldn't do. Jealousy had no place in the situation here. She *must* get used to thinking of Hugh in an impersonal way, as the head of the important company she worked for—nothing more. If she gave in to the fantasy that had seduced her last night he would guess. He would smile very kindly at her and say, 'Sorry, Lissa, nothing doing.' And then she would want to die.

'Would you like to look round the garden—to put in time until Hugh returns?' Monique said.

'I'd love to.' Lissa dragged her thoughts back to reality. 'My mother's a keen gardener and she'll be interested to hear what you grow in Paris.'

The garden was formal, with shrubs and flower-beds. 'Marie's husband, Henri, looks after it all for us,' Monique said. 'I'm no gardener, I'm afraid— I'm better at painting flowers than growing them.'

'Oh, did you paint the flower pictures in the bedroom? I've been admiring them—they're beautiful.'

'Very much in the amateur class.' Monique smiled ruefully. 'But I'm so happy now I can spend time painting—something I've always wanted to do.'

She walked on in silence for a while and Lissa wondered if she was remembering a time when her love of painting had been frustrated. Perhaps Hugh's father hadn't been very sympathetic about art. A man who had founded a company like Winchester Electronics must have had his life bounded by business affairs. Like his son.

They strolled on together and Monique pointed out an early-flowering shrub or two. 'The spring flowers are all over,' she said. 'They come along a little earlier here than in England—or rather, in the part of England where I used to live.'

'In the south?' Lissa enquired politely. She thought that her hostess seemed rather abstracted.

'Oh, yes, in the south. Home counties, of course.' There was a touch of acid in the pleasant voice and Lissa realised that she had been tactless. Monique wouldn't want to be reminded of what had probably been a none too happy life with Hugh's father in a land not her own.

She tried to think of something to say, but her hostess went on, 'Do I sound bitter? I shouldn't be, I suppose, I had a lovely house and a wonderful son to bring up. But my first marriage was not very happy.' She sighed. 'I expect a lot of it was my own fault.' She went on quickly, 'Now, tell me about your home, Lissa. Do you live with your parents?'

Lissa jumped eagerly at the change of subject and talked warmly about her home in Streatham, about her father, who was an accountant with a London firm and her mother, who was getting more and more involved with her Oxfam work. 'They're having a holiday in America just now, celebrating their silver wedding anniversary.'

'How very nice! Hugh said something on the phone about your parents being away. He was quite perturbed about your having nowhere to go when you had your accident.' Lissa thought she caught a sideways, questioning glance, but she didn't enlarge on what she had said. Without going into details of exactly what had happened, she couldn't explain any further, and she certainly didn't want to do that.

'They're having a grand time,' she said. 'I telephoned them from the nursing home. I wonder if I might phone again later in the day—they will still be asleep now—and let them know where I am? I wasn't quite sure when I spoke to them...'

The words trailed off as the sound of a car in the drive made them both look round and Monique said, 'Ah, this will be Hugh now, I expect.' She glanced uncertainly at Lissa, stretched out a hand and dropped it again. In a slightly embarrassed voice she said, 'You mustn't mind about Carolyn, Lissa. Hugh has known her ever since she was a child. Come along, let's go and meet him.'

She hurried off across the lawn and Lissa followed more slowly. What was all that about? Why should Hugh's mother think she would 'mind' about Carolyn and Hugh? Had she shown too plainly last night that she was eaten up with jealousy? Oh, surely not. There was only one other possibility, which was that Hugh's parents believed that she had been brought here as Hugh's girlfriend, rather than his business associate. Monsieur Delage's remark about *'coup de foudre'* would then make sense.

If that was true it put her in a horribly false position and she must tackle Hugh about it as soon as possible. Firming her mouth and lifting her chin a little, she went to meet him.

A sporty black Renault pulled up in front of the house and Hugh levered himself out. In spite of her good resolutions, Lissa's heart gave a great lunge at the sight of him. He looked gorgeous, so long and lean and fit, with the sunshine burnishing his black hair and making it shine like ebony. He threw an arm round his mother's waist and dropped a kiss on her forehead. 'Here I am, Maman, the prodigal son returns.'

As Lissa came up to them he greeted her with a friendly smile. 'Hello, sweetheart, had a good sleep?' He circled her waist with his other arm. Thus linked the three of them went into the house. Monique was saying something to Hugh about the gallery and asking if he had left before Claude arrived this morning. Lissa hardly noticed what they were saying; she was much too aware of the pressure of his hand at her waist. She gave her shoulders a little shake and the pressure tightened.

In the hall Monique drew away and Hugh released Lissa, giving her an odd look, straight into her eyes, which might have meant anything—or nothing. 'Any coffee going, Maman?' he enquired. 'I mustn't linger, though, I want to get down to work.'

His mother said, 'I'll ask Katrine to bring some coffee to your study, shall I? For both of you?'

'Oh, yes, certainly. I shall need Lissa there with me.'

'Of course.' His mother's mouth gave an undeniable twitch at the corners as she went off towards the kitchen quarters.

Hugh stood smiling down at Lissa. 'Ready for work, Lissa? Are you fully recovered?'

'Fully, thank you,' she said composedly. 'I went to your office earlier on, but of course you weren't there.' Oh, dear, she had made that sound almost like a reproach.

'No, I wasn't, was I?' There was a touch of mockery in his voice. For a moment they stared at each other, his silver-grey eyes creasing at the corners with amusement, hers wide with puzzlement. She was beginning to feel very much out of her depth here.

His smile disappeared. His eyes narrowed, the ridiculously long lashes veiling them. He said slowly, 'You're too pretty to be cooped up in an office, Lissa. I'm not sure that I can...' He stopped, frowning. 'Oh, come along,' he said impatiently, and set off at a great pace across the hall.

In the office he pulled off his light jacket and flung himself into a chair behind the desk. He began to sort through the papers and folders there while Lissa stood and watched him, trying to nerve herself to say what she had to say.

'Well, sit down, sit down,' he told her rather irritably, waving towards a chair on the opposite side of the desk.

Lissa continued to stand, her fingers closing on the back of the chair. 'Mr Winchester...' she began.

'Hugh,' he corrected without looking up.

She ignored that. 'Mr Winchester,' she repeated, 'there's something I must say before I start working for you.'

Something in her voice must have got through to him, for he did look up then, a frown settling between his dark brows. 'Well?'

She drew in a quick breath. 'I want to know what you have told your mother about what happened in London. About Paul and me. She seems to think...'

Oh, lord, she shouldn't have begun like that. She quailed at the look of fury that settled on Hugh's features—cold, frozen fury that was so much worse than the fiery sort.

'I'm not in the habit of regaling my mother with squalid office gossip,' he said icily.

'But she thinks——' Lissa tried again.

Again he cut her off. 'People will think what they choose to think. I've told my mother you've come here to work for me. What more would you like me to say? I doubt if it would interest her if I told her you'd fallen for my stepbrother and I thought fit to tear you away from him.' The sarcasm in his voice cut like a sharp knife.

'But that isn't what I meant at all,' she said unhappily. The way he twisted everything round was maddening.

'Very well, what *did* you mean, then? Perhaps you'll explain. And make it snappy—I want to get started with the work.'

What could she say? That his mother seemed to think he'd brought her here as his girlfriend? She remembered what he had said about cradle-snatching and could imagine how he would take *that*. He would either laugh at her or cut her to bits with his sarcasm. She couldn't risk either.

Katrine came in then with the coffee, which seemed to provide a full stop to the matter.

'Oh, never mind, it doesn't matter,' she said, and sat down in the chair he had indicated. 'I'm sorry I said anything. Now, perhaps you'll tell me what you want me to do.'

He fixed his gaze on her for a moment, still frowning. Then he shrugged slightly and said, 'Perhaps first you'd better tell me exactly what you've been doing in London. Secretarial work, was it?'

She shook her head. 'No, I was Paul's assistant on the office equipment side of the business. I trained in business management, not in secretarial work, but I did learn typing as well—it's always useful.'

'Paul's assistant? And what exactly did that comprise?' He slanted her an ironic glance. 'I mean *company* work, of course.'

Lissa stiffened slightly but decided to ignore that. Let him think what he liked. What did it matter to her what he thought?

She drank her coffee before she answered and then she said coolly, 'There was always plenty to do. I interviewed customers and manufacturers, sometimes travelled to see them. I kept the files and order-books up to date, checked on delivery times— the hundred and one things that come up in a marketing department.'

'In other words, you were doing Paul's job for him.'

'Oh, no, that's not fair,' she said quickly. Although, when she came to think of it, it was probably true. Paul had certainly been out of the office recently more than he'd been in it. 'You're marvellous,' he'd said to her often, 'you keep things on the move.' She'd been flattered and pleased and it hadn't occurred to her that he'd been leaning much too hard on her. 'I've enjoyed the work. Although I'd really have preferred to be on the technical side, but I haven't had any training in computing. I planned to start at an evening class in September.'

He was looking hard at her while she spoke. Now he said, 'You can scrub the evening classes. I'll teach you all you need to know in half the time.' A small grin hovered round his mouth. 'Personal instruction—one to one. There's nothing to touch it.'

'Thank you, Mr Winchester,' Lissa said composedly. 'It's very good of you.'

He threw her an exasperated look. 'I've told you to drop the "Mr Winchester", Lissa. Why won't you, for Pete's sake?'

She couldn't sit still any longer while he glared at her as if she were a specimen on a glass slide. She got up and walked to the window and looked out between the slats of the Venetian blind. This was an opportunity not to be missed—she simply must tackle him now.

She kept her eyes straight ahead. 'I tried to tell you before, but you deliberately misunderstood. The fact is, I feel in a false position here. It's obvious that your mother—and Monsieur Delage as well—think that the work thing is just an excuse— that you brought me as as—as——' she floundered and then went on determinedly '—as your girlfriend or—or something. It puts me in such a difficult position. I think it's up to you to make it quite clear to them that it isn't true.'

She heard him push his chair back and then he was standing beside her at the window, so close that his arm brushed against hers. She moved away slightly, her knees rubbery, feeling appalled at the physical effect the man had on her.

He wasn't affected in the least, she thought, glancing up at his hard profile, the dark brows drawn together in frowning concentration. She waited to hear what he had to say, and when he spoke at last it wasn't at all what she had expected.

'There's something I've got to tell you. I'd hoped to leave it until we'd got some work done, but as you've brought the matter up you'd better know now.'

She turned to him, eyes wide. 'I don't understand...'

'No, of course you don't.' He was impatient now. 'I haven't told you yet. Come and sit down and listen.' He put an arm round her shoulders to turn her back to her chair. At the touch of his hands through the thin stuff of her blouse she shivered and drew away.

He released her immediately, almost pushed her away. 'You *have* got the Paul bug badly, haven't you? Can't you even bear another man's touch?' He didn't wait for an answer, but pulled out a chair and pushed her roughly into it.

'Now listen to me,' he said, leaning back against the desk, arms folded. 'I've got a problem and I'm relying on you to help me with it.'

Lissa sat up straight, her mouth firm. She didn't take aggression well, and wasn't disposed to agree to anything more he asked of her. 'Well?' she said coldly.

He glanced at her and looked away. 'It's about Carolyn.'

This was the last thing Lissa had expected, and she certainly wasn't going to get involved in the details of the man's love life. 'I don't think I can——' she began.

'Oh, shut up and listen,' he barked. 'The fact is that Carolyn is as jealous as hell—of you.'

Lissa's lips twisted. '"Curiouser and curiouser,"' she quoted.

'Is it?' he said darkly. 'It seems quite reasonable to me. I arrive here with a particularly lovely girl and say I've brought her to work with me. Naturally, Carolyn puts the obvious construction on it.'

A particularly lovely girl! He made it sound almost like an insult. She said, 'As your mother did—and Monsieur Delage? That's what I told you——'

'Yes, I know damn well what you told me.' He ran his fingers through his dark hair in frustration. Lissa could have laughed if she hadn't felt so angry. For the first time, this reasonable, logical individual had actually lost his cool!

'Well, I don't see much of a problem,' she said. 'What do you want me to do—disclaim all rights to your—er—affections?'

He glared at her. 'Trust a female to get everything beautifully mixed up,' he said savagely. He pulled up a chair close to hers. 'Now listen, woman, and don't interrupt.'

Lissa folded her hands on her lap and tried to look completely uninterested.

'The fact is,' Hugh began, 'that Carolyn thinks she has a claim to my time—and to me.' He grimaced. 'Her father was my godfather and my greatest friend—he gave me all the things that my own father never did: affection, advice, encouragement, understanding. When he died in a car accident three years ago it was the greatest blow I'd suffered in my life. Carolyn was eighteen then— just finished school, very pretty and vulnerable. She was heartbroken and alone. Her father hadn't left her much money—he was a lecturer and they don't amass fortunes. Her mother had walked out on the family some time previously. Carolyn turned to me and I wanted to do what I could to help, for her father's sake as much as hers. After various——' he paused slightly '—ups and downs, I arranged a job in Claude's gallery for her—nothing too demanding—and got her digs with a nice family in Paris.'

He paused, looking very faintly uncomfortable. 'The trouble is that she's been building up all sorts of fantasies about me. You know the theory about the patient falling in love with her psychiatrist? That's obviously what's happened. Now she's taking it for granted that I intend to marry her.'

He got up and paced to the window and stood looking out moodily. 'I've had a suspicion that something like this was happening. Every time I came here she would turn to me for all sorts of things, demanding my time and attention. I couldn't bring myself to brush her off. Poor, foolish little Carolyn, I care a lot about her, but I certainly don't intend to marry her—or anyone else,' he added, turning on Lissa belligerently.

She glared back at him. 'Don't shout at me. *I'm* not expecting you to marry me.'

He came back and sank into his chair. 'I'm sorry, Lissa, I got a bit carried away. All I want is to be left alone to get on with my work. Romantic complications are out, so far as I'm concerned. The last thing I need is to have a lovesick maiden hanging round my neck.'

She eyed him critically. 'For such a logical man, you seem to have been somewhat illogical. Surely a little foresight would have avoided the problem.' After the way he had treated her it was nice to feel a small sense of triumph. 'But I really don't see how I can help you.'

'You can, Lissa—you can. You can play along with what I let Carolyn believe last night.'

Shocked surprise took her by the throat. 'You told Carolyn that I—that we——' she swallowed '—that we're sleeping together?'

'That's what she believes and it seemed logical to let her believe it. I thought it would be kinder to let her think there was another girl, rather than give her a brutal brush-off, poor kid. She's been through a bad time and I don't want to hurt her more than I need.'

Lissa jumped to her feet, hot anger seething inside her. 'How dare you? What an unforgivable thing to do! You'd no right, no right at all . . .' Her voice rose to a screech and then, humiliatingly, cracked.

He reached up and took both her hands in his. 'Cool it, Lissa, it's not the end of the world. It seemed the only reasonable thing to do.'

'Reasonable!' she flared at him. 'Logical! What kind of a man are you to talk about being reasonable when you've—you've . . .?' She shook her arms but didn't manage to disengage her hands from his.

'I've what?' he said mildly. 'I've paid you the compliment of letting it be thought that I'm in love with you. And it is a compliment, I assure you. Love is a word that I've never used in my—dealings with your sex.' He gripped her hands harder. 'All I'm asking of you is not to deny it if the matter should arise. I'm pleading with you, Lissa, out of the goodness of your heart.' He pulled a face at the corny expression. 'After all, Carolyn need never know the truth—that you're carrying a torch for Paul.'

Paul again! 'How does Paul come into this?'

For a moment he looked disconcerted. Then he said hastily, letting go of her hands, 'Of course he doesn't—it was merely something that occurred to me. What about it, Lissa? Will you back me up? You'd be doing the child—and me—a great kindness. She'd be let down gently and no doubt would soon find a nice young man to fall in love with and——'

'And you would be free to get on with your precious work and bother no more about other people's feelings?' She gazed up at him incredulously. 'You really are—are the limit,' she ended up weakly.

The grey eyes softened as he sensed success. 'And you really are a nice girl, Lissa. And, of course, we probably won't ever need to put on an act. I don't suppose we shall see very much of Carolyn when we're together. I'm very grateful to you.'

'So you should be,' she said tartly. 'I don't know why I should be agreeing to pretend I'm in love with you.'

'Would it be so very difficult?' he mocked.

'Almost impossible,' she retorted. If she had to lie she might as well make it as convincing as she could. 'You're not my type at all. I'm sorry for any girl who falls in love with you—that's why I'm agreeing to get you off the hook with Carolyn— for her sake, not yours.'

'I appreciate that,' he said almost humbly, and he was serious now, not mocking, or teasing, or angry. They were meeting on common ground; for the first time he was treating her as an equal, and Lissa was conscious of a small thrill of satisfaction.

'Poor Carolyn,' she sighed, getting to her feet. As he rose beside her she felt again, stronger than ever, the magnetic attraction of the man, the attraction that she must resist at all costs, or she would be in the same boat as Carolyn. She glanced up at him and said casually, 'Don't you intend to marry—ever?'

His mouth went down at the corners as he shook his head. 'Statistics don't exactly encourage one, do they? I saw enough of marriage as a child. I grew up watching my parents tear each other to pieces. Although——' he paused, looking thoughtful '—my mother certainly seems to be very happy with her second venture. But no.' He shook his head decisively. 'I worked out some time ago that marriage isn't for me. A long-term understanding with no strings—that's the logical solution these days.'

'And has it struck you that one of these days your precious logic won't be enough to keep you out of danger?'

He gave her a suspicious look. 'Don't take the mickey, Lissa. Being my guinea-pig doesn't give you that excuse.'

'Oh, I wouldn't dare, Mr Winchester,' she murmured meekly, slanting a glance up at him as she started to walk towards the computer table.

He put both hands on her shoulders and turned her to face him. 'Little devil. You did that deliberately, didn't you?' He shook her none too gently. '*Didn't* you?'

'Did what deliberately?' Sparkling green eyes searched his. 'Let me *go*!' She flapped her arms helplessly.

His grip tightened. 'You know damn well "what". Haven't you learned anything about men like me—the kind of men it's dangerous to flirt with?'

Her stomach twisted as his face came close, the steely eyes glittering into hers. 'I'm not flirting,' she gasped. 'It's just that—that I find you rather overwhelming, and I don't like being over-whelmed. So I try to—to lighten the atmosphere a little, that's all.'

'I—see,' he murmured, his mouth close to hers. 'Well, next time you try to lighten the atmosphere just give a thought to what might happen—*this*.'

His mouth closed on hers and Lissa felt a deep shiver pass through her. At first his kiss was hard and she knew he had intended a punishment. Then it changed and his lips moved gently, caressingly on hers. 'Nice—very, very nice,' he murmured against her mouth.

Oh, it *was* nice—what a stupid word! It wasn't merely nice, it was the most wonderful experience she had ever known. No other kiss had made the floor move beneath her feet, had sent the blood rushing round her body in an unstoppable torrent.

His arms dropped to her waist, pulling her against him, and her hands went up of their own accord to close round his neck. She was burning, melting, and her lips opened to the pressure of his tongue as the kiss became more intimate, more de-manding. He moved against her and she felt the urgency in his hard, dynamic body. Her head was spinning but somehow she clung on to a vestige of sanity.

She pulled her mouth from his. 'No—please——' she gasped.

He let her go immediately and she staggered back to her chair, her breath coming in shallow gasps. Hugh stood by the window, his back to her; he pulled up the Venetian blind with an impatient tug and the slats clattered noisily in the quiet room. Then he flung up the bottom sash of the window. 'Let some fresh air in,' he muttered.

When he turned round again Lissa met his sombre gaze without flinching. She had made up her mind what to say without even thinking about it. 'I don't think it's going to work—my being here,' she said tightly. 'I'd like to leave as soon as possible.'

'Why?' he demanded curtly.

She lifted her hands and dropped them again. 'Isn't it obvious?'

'Because I kissed you?' He laughed harshly. 'You asked for it, you know—fluttering those long lashes at me. Is that how you looked at Paul?'

Anger began to take over. 'What's Paul got to do with it?' she demanded. 'You seem to have Paul on the brain. Can't we forget Paul?'

He shrugged and said slowly, deliberately, 'There's one thing I've just proved—it may be possible to make *you* forget Paul.'

She turned on him furiously. 'So this is an experiment, is it? You're trying to put me off Paul?'

'If you like. I think I should be doing you a favour.' The grey eyes were cold as mountain pools. He picked up a blue ring-file from the desk and held it out to her. 'Suppose you start tackling the work now? That's the really important thing.'

Lissa stared down at the file he was holding. She thought that his hand wasn't quite steady, but she must be imagining that. She was still trembling herself but surely he wouldn't have been disturbed by a mere kiss.

She had to choose at this moment. She could stay and endure certain heartache. Or she could insist on leaving the company here and now—*and never see him again*. That was the logical, reasonable thing to do, wasn't it?

She held out her hand and took the blue folder from him and he nodded, smiling faintly, as if he had proved something. Which he had, the brute. He had proved that when it came to a contest of wills he would always win. She sank into her chair, feeling as if she had fought some great battle—and lost.

He stood for a moment beside her chair and she was alarmingly conscious of his long, firm body beneath the close-fitting trousers and thin cotton shirt. She caught a faint whiff of masculine cologne and for a second she was back in his arms, his mouth on hers. She closed her eyes and fought against a rising tide of desire.

'I'll come back later and see how you're getting on,' he said. 'Good luck.'

She wasn't sure whether he put his hand on her shoulder for a fleeting moment before he walked out of the office. Perhaps she had imagined it. Yes, she must have imagined it, she told herself firmly.

Lissa drew in a deep breath, let it out again, and opened the blue ring-file.

CHAPTER FIVE

IT WAS nearly half an hour before Hugh came back into the office. Lissa looked up and smiled distantly as he sat down in the chair beside her, merely acknowledging his presence. From now on, she had decided, everything would be on a business basis when they were together in the office. What he had in mind for the times they were with his mother and Claude she hadn't had the courage to consider yet.

He said, 'I've been for a walk in the garden. Sorry about——' he waved a hand vaguely '—all that. Am I forgiven, and can we get on with the work now?'

Lissa had never admired people who took umbrage and sulked. What he had just said was as near to an apology as she was going to get.

She nodded briefly. 'Yes, Mr Winchester.'

'Hugh,' he reminded her.

'OK, then—Hugh,' she said sturdily. She looked down at the blue ring-file. 'I've read most of the introduction. Is this the computer I've got to try to understand?'

He put a hand lovingly on the top of the VDU connected to the compact new computer on the table before her. 'This is the little beauty. We hope to get it on the market in the autumn or early next year.'

Lissa looked at his hand with the long, sensitive fingers and felt her stomach contract. If he had touched her as tenderly as he touched his computer that would have been bliss, she thought, and immediately dragged her mind back to the work in hand.

'Did you do all the design and everything yourself?' she enquired.

'Oh, lord, no. I'd have to be Superman to put in the time required. I've got a company to run—the technical stuff is really a sideline for me, although sometimes I wish it weren't. I've got an excellent team—they're all based in Dorset, at the factory. The London office is mainly concerned with sales.' He paused, frowning slightly. 'I suppose I should warn you—as you're employed on the office equipment side of the business—that I'm planning to sell off that side in the near future.'

'Oh!' That was a blow. 'Where does that leave the staff?'

The long mouth twisted into a sneer. 'Worried about Paul? I shouldn't bother—Paul is well able to look after himself. Selfishness is second nature with Paul. He'll always look after number one.'

Suddenly she hated the way he spoke of Paul—it seemed to—to diminish him, make him almost petty. She said quite heatedly, 'I really don't think you're fair to Paul. I got to know him well when I was working with him and he's a really nice person—kind, and—and understanding. Just because he likes to have fun, that doesn't make him...'

Her voice faltered and died away as she saw the coldly furious expression that came to Hugh's face, the way his mouth thinned into a hard line.

She swallowed. 'I'm sorry—it isn't my business. And anyway, I was thinking about my own job.'

He got up, walked to the window, and stood there in silence. She looked miserably at his straight back. Why had she had to stick up for Paul like that? She might have guessed it would antagonise him.

But when he came back and sat down again his face had cleared. 'No problem. I'd like to keep you working with me. When we get back to England I'll take you along to Dorset to see the set-up there, and you can meet the team. You'll like Joe Kewley, who does all the programming for us—he a wizard. If you want to learn programming he's your man. How about it?'

'Sounds interesting,' she said composedly. She wouldn't let him see how the idea thrilled her. If they were working together maybe he'd change, maybe he'd fall in love with her. It wasn't much of a hope, but it was something to hang on to.

'You'd be in on the launch too—it's going to be quite an exciting time.' His eyes shone with enthusiasm. 'But there's a lot of preliminary work to be done before that. One of the important things, to my mind, is to get a really super manual. I've been working on it for weeks and the result is what you're holding in your hand.'

She glanced up at him as he sat beside her. This was where his real interest lay—not in personalities.

'The idea,' he went on, grey eyes glinting, 'is to market the machine complete with all its own software. The software will be compatible, of course, with other computers, but the thing is that the buyer will start off with a completely self-contained working office environment. Do you get the idea?'

'I—think so.' Lissa hadn't quite followed what he'd been saying, but perhaps the manual would make all clear. 'What particular market are we targeting?'

He nodded approvingly. 'Ah, there speaks the professional! We have in mind the rather older man or woman who is thinking of starting up a new business. The young ones have it all at their fingertips, but for someone older—possibly retired from another job—the computer is often a bogeyman. He—she—knows that a micro would be invaluable if only it didn't seem so complicated and time-consuming to learn how to use it.'

'And I'm to pretend to be this man—er—woman?'

'Right!'

'I see.' Lissa looked thoughtful. 'Well, the first thing is to imagine myself into the part. What's my name?'

Hugh blinked. Then he saw the dimple flickering in her cheek and shrugged tolerantly. 'Technology with a human face, eh? OK, shall we say Smith?'

'Right. I'm Mrs Smith, a forty-year-old housewife whose children have just left home. My husband is immersed in his job and I'm bored and lonely so I'm thinking of starting my own business. What sort of a business do I mean to start?'

Lissa could see that this playful approach to Hugh's beloved work discipline was new to him, but he joined in the game with good grace. 'Weell, let's say something you can do from home. Something you're good at and enjoy. How about some sort of cookery?'

She pulled a face at him. 'Back to the old role-playing! Never mind. I'm going to make gourmet dishes and sell them to local shops. Go on.'

He stroked his chin. 'Let's say your son's just left for university but on his bedroom table is his pride and joy—his new micro. This.' He patted the machine on the table. 'Before he leaves he says, "Why not use my micro for your new venture, Mummy dear. Feel free."'

Lissa giggled. 'He'd be more likely to lock it up in a cupboard.'

'Ah, but this is a nice young man and he loves his mum.'

'OK,' she said, 'I'll try to go along with that. So I tell him I don't know a thing about micros and they terrify me.'

'"Simple," he says. "Just read the book and all will be revealed. You'll get the hang in no time, you clever old Mum."'

Lissa said slowly, 'I'd like a son like that some day.'

There was a small silence and she felt Hugh's eyes on her. He was probably very bored by her frivolous approach. She said brightly, 'OK. I'm Mrs Smith and you're going to throw me in at the deep end, clutching your new manual, and see whether I sink or swim. Charming! I see now where the guinea-pig idea comes in.'

Hugh frowned. 'We've had some fun about it, Lissa, but the project's dead serious to me. I'm used to talking computer jargon to people who understand it, so that makes it difficult to get inside the mind of someone who's quite new to technology, people bright enough to start small businesses but who jib at the thought of learning about computers.'

'Yes, I see,' Lissa said. 'But do you think *I'm* bright enough?'

His strange silver-grey eyes moved over her face slowly, assessingly, for some reason coming to rest on her mouth. 'Of course you are. You're just what I need.'

The deep, lazy voice seemed to touch a chord low inside her and set it vibrating. *You're just what I need!* She felt the heat in her face and turned away quickly. 'That's fine, then,' she said calmly. 'It sounds quite a challenge. I can't wait to get going.'

He leaned back in his chair, watching her face intently. 'Just why are you keen on learning computing, Lissa?'

'Oh, I don't know. Why do certain things appeal to certain people? Technology's the future, and I don't intend to be left out of the future. For a start, if I'm any good at it I might be able to get a transfer to the technical side of the company. It would be more interesting than selling executive swivel chairs or split-level work-stations.'

He burst out laughing at that and then became serious again. 'You're ambitious, are you?'

'Certainly. You'll be making me a director one of these days,' she said airily. 'Ten years from now, perhaps. I'll be thirty-two then, is that too young for a company director?'

He pretended to consider. 'I suppose not. But you'll be married with a family long before then.'

'Company directors sometimes get married. Even female company directors.'

Suddenly he seemed to be bored with the conversation. He got up and went to his own desk on the opposite side of the room. 'Let's get on, then, shall we?' he said.

Lissa turned to the new computer. Her mouth twisted into a wry smile—she thought it would be nice if she could manage to fall in love with it, as Hugh obviously had done.

'I think,' Monique said, regarding her son sternly across the breakfast table five days later, 'that it is time you gave Lissa a break. You've both been working every hour of the day, and the child is looking quite exhausted.'

Hugh put down his coffee-cup and regarded Lissa, lips pursed, head on one side. '*Are* you exhausted, Lissa?'

Lissa looked down at her plate with a small smile. She found it better not to meet Hugh's eyes when it wasn't strictly necessary.

She had an uneasy feeling that his mother was watching them, puzzled as to exactly what their relationship was, and she was fairly sure that he hadn't told her of his plan to discourage Carolyn.

To Lissa's relief it hadn't been necessary to make any change in the way she behaved towards Hugh. In fact, once the work of the day was finished neither she nor his parents saw very much of him. After dinner he retired once again to his office and Lissa made a point of going to bed early so that they didn't meet again until the next morning.

In the office Hugh had carefully avoided personalities, after that first day. But even though he was merely explaining to her some point in his manual which puzzled her, he had a habit of looking intently at her in a way that set her nerves jangling. She wondered if he did it on purpose, if he was just amusing himself at her expense. He must know that his lazy, challenging stare affected her in a way that had nothing to do with the matter under discussion.

Now, in answer to his quizzical, '*Are* you exhausted, Lissa?' she murmured, 'I'm fine, thanks.'

'There you are, Maman, Lissa is fine. And we've got a lot of work to get through. So I'm afraid joining the tourist trail in Paris is out for today. Tomorrow, perhaps,' he added vaguely, and Lissa saw that his mind had already switched on to the day's work ahead.

The room that Hugh used as an office seemed smaller than usual this morning. Warmer, too. Lissa sat before the computer screen and the tiny words and symbols glared back at her. The cursor—that little white block that indicated where she was on the screen—flashed and blinked in a way that began to feel almost painful. After an hour, a dull ache began to spread across her forehead and the cursor danced mockingly before her eyes.

She looked over her shoulder to where Hugh was working at the desk. 'Hugh . . .'

He raised his head with the faint frown that always touched his brow whenever she had to disturb him in his thoughts.

'Is it possible to stop the cursor from flashing?' Lissa said. 'It's driving me crazy.'

He came across the room and stood behind her chair, looking into the screen.

'Yes, I see what you mean, it hadn't struck me before. I wonder . . .' His voice trailed off.

He was leaning down and his mouth was very close to the top of her head. She could feel his breath on her forehead and her heart started its now familiar tap-dance.

She stared straight ahead, waiting for him to go on. But he seemed to have run out of ideas. Finally he said, 'What do you put on your hair?'

'Shampoo,' she said. 'Tiki, if you're interested. I use that brand because it doesn't involve experiments on animals. Why, does the smell offend you?'

'On the contrary,' he said smoothly. 'I find it very—er—stimulating.' He gripped the back of her swivel chair and swung it round.

'Look at me, Lissa,' he said, as she performed her usual trick of fixing her gaze anywhere but on his intent grey eyes.

She looked up—a long way up—and eventually their eyes met. It felt to Lissa as if she had encountered a live electric current. To her intense annoyance the blood left her face and then rushed back again. She couldn't remember blushing like that ever before.

Somehow she managed to hold his look, willing herself not to drop her eyes. Amazingly, it was Hugh whose eyes moved first, searching her cheeks and then her mouth, in a puzzled sort of way. At last he said, 'Yes, I believe Maman was right, I think I have been working you too hard. I shouldn't like to turn my guinea-pig into a work-horse. You've tackled the job splendidly and we're ahead of the deadline. Let's go and sample the delights of the great capital city—how does that appeal?'

'Very much,' Lissa said quietly, hiding the excitement that suddenly banished her tiredness.

'Good, let's go, then. Outside in the car in five minutes?'

It sounded like an order, the way he'd said it. Obviously he didn't particularly want to take her out, he was merely indulging his mother's wishes. And perhaps he thought she looked a trifle jaded and wasn't going to keep up the pace he had set.

'*Fifteen* minutes,' Lissa said firmly. She stood up, looking down at her neat navy skirt and white blouse. 'I can't go into Paris like this.'

He surveyed her impatiently. 'You look all right to me.'

She smiled sweetly, but not quite into his eyes. 'Thanks very much—if that's a compliment. All the same, I should like to change. Outside in the car in—say—fifteen minutes?' She mimicked his brisk, authoritative tone and swept out of the room.

In the bedroom she surveyed the clothes she had chosen for the Scottish trip. If only she'd known she was coming to Paris she would have packed a few much more exciting garments. But these would have to do for the moment. The cream linen suit was the only possible choice. She took it from its hanger and selected a crêpe de Chine blouse in a buttery caramel colour. Stripping off her office clothes, she slipped her arms into the soft crêpe of the blouse, aware of a rising feeling of excitement. Even if Hugh was taking her out under protest, at least he *was* taking her out, and she was determined to enjoy her first sight of Paris.

In the office she had been wearing her tawny curls tied back demurely, but now she sat at the dressing-table and pulled off the black ribbon, running her fingers through her hair to produce an effect that was casual and, she thought, just a little dashing. It was curious how a hairstyle did something for one's confidence. Glancing at her watch, she went out to join Hugh.

She found him leaning on the bonnet of his black Renault, looking up into the sky as if he was resigned to waiting a long, long time.

'Fourteen minutes flat,' Lissa said cheerfully.

He lowered his head and examined her slowly from her delicately untidy hairstyle to her neat bronze sandals.

'Hm—very erotic,' he mused, opening the car door for her.

'Erotic? What are you talking about?' Lissa gasped.

He slipped into the driving seat and treated her to an ironic glance. 'What poet was it who said, "A sweet disorder in the dress kindles in clothes a wantonness"? I suppose the same applies to hair.' He put out a finger and touched a stray curl that had wandered on to her cheek. 'It puts a man in mind of tumbled pillows and two heaps of clothes on the floor.'

Lissa looked straight ahead, her pulse jumping erratically. 'I can't help it if your mind works like that.'

'Relax, sweetheart,' he said lazily, turning the ignition key. 'All men's minds work like that. Haven't you noticed?'

She slanted a glance at him as the car joined the traffic on the main road. 'Is this the whiter-than-white knight who rescued me from a fate worse than death in the office in London?'

She expected him to bark at her, or at least frown her into silence. But instead he said, so softly that she could only just hear the words above the noise of the traffic, 'I could give you an answer to that if we were in a less public place.'

Lissa was reduced to silence, a silence that seemed to vibrate urgently inside her with the engine of the car. When she was capable of speech again she said brightly, 'Where are we going?'

'First of all we'll find somewhere to park the car—which may be a major problem, although I hope not. After that—well, we'll just amuse ourselves as the spirit takes us. We'll be going through a tunnel before very long. Look out for the view on the other side. It's only fleeting, but well worth seeing.'

From that Lissa gathered that Hugh was going to do his best to entertain her. Probably his mildly flirtatious remarks were all part of the package—for entertainment only. The fleeting view he had promised her made her catch her breath when it appeared. It was as if all the city were spread out below, quivering in the heat-haze that hung over everything.

'Beautiful!' Lissa murmured, her eyes taking in with delight the wide patchwork of classically elegant buildings with their ruler-straight rows of windows, the scattered bunches of trees, the spire of a church. 'Oh, and the Eiffel Tower over there in the distance—now I *know* I'm in Paris. And the river winding in and out, with all those little bridges. It looks like a necklace of diamonds.' Excitement bubbled in her voice. 'How absolutely super to see

Paris for the first time on such a heavenly day—
I'm absolutely thrilled. Thank you for bringing me.'

Hugh didn't move his eyes from the busy road.
But he took his right hand off the wheel and
touched her knee. 'Thank you for coming,' he said,
very low.

Oh, heavens! Surely only a Frenchman could say
those words in just that velvety, caressing tone, and
it came home to Lissa for the first time that Hugh
was half-French. Her toes curled up inside her
bronze sandals. The man could be dynamite if he
chose; she didn't know how she was going to hide
the way she was beginning to feel about him.
Perhaps she wouldn't hide it, she thought dizzily.
Perhaps she would let Paris work its subtle, romantic magic.

As if Paris were deliberately showing its other
side, the car park Hugh found was an enormous
underground affair, dingy and dark and echoing.
Lissa stopped counting the number of floors, as
they went deeper and deeper—into the middle of
the earth, it seemed. When a vacant space eventually appeared and Hugh drove into it and shut off
the engine, it was quite an effort to laugh and say,
'I certainly wouldn't like to come down here alone—
it's creepy.'

Hugh turned to her. 'You're not alone, little girl.
I'll look after you. Not for the first time,' he added
with a chuckle. 'You'd better leave your jacket in
the car—you don't want to carry it around with
you all day, and it's going to be a real sizzler.'

Lissa shivered. 'I'm freezing,' she objected.

'You'll be burning when we get up aloft,' he insisted. 'Come on, off with it.' He reached over and

unclipped her seatbelt and began to unfasten the buttons of her jacket.

Lissa sat very still as she felt his hands against the swell of her breast under the light jacket, and suddenly she *was* burning. The blood surged into her cheeks and she was thankful for the darkness around. She let Hugh ease the sleeves of the jacket off her shoulders and when his hand came to rest on her neck, underneath the fall of curls, she made no resistance.

'Not exactly the most romantic part of Paris, perhaps,' he murmured, close to her ear. He turned her face towards him, his hand under her chin, and when he began to kiss her she melted into his arms.

His lips gentled her mouth, brushing over it backwards and forwards, and Lissa parted her own lips to allow him entrance. For a few blissful moments, in the near darkness, she clung to him as his arm drew her close and his kiss became deeper and more intimate until a shudder passed through her and she had enough wits left to pull away from him.

He let her go slowly and reluctantly. 'I suppose you're right,' he said with a sigh. He picked up a curl that had drifted over her cheek and wound it round his finger. 'Did that answer the question you asked me earlier? I'm the same man that rescued you from Paul, but unlike Paul I do have a few standards left—I hope. So——' he leaned across and pushed open the car door on her side '—the safest thing is to remove ourselves from temptation and sample the delights of Paris.'

Lissa's knees were wobbly as she got out of the car. Hugh was simply amusing himself with a kiss now and again while she was falling more in love with him every moment.

In the dark intimacy of the car she had been afraid that her emotions might run away with her, but once they were back at ground level and had emerged into the sun-soaked boulevard the infectious gaiety of the city took over.

Hugh linked his arm with hers and said, 'Is there anything particular you want to see?'

Lissa dredged her memory for everything she had heard and read and seen on TV about Paris. 'Of course,' she said airily, ticking them off on her fingers. 'Notre Dame and the Louvre and the Opéra and the Pompidou Centre and Montmartre and the Tuileries and the quayside bookstalls and the chic shops——'

'Stop!' Hugh shook her arm. 'My feet are killing me at the prospect. Let's go and have a nice, long cool drink first. Yes?'

'Whatever you say,' Lissa agreed. She would have agreed to anything he suggested. This was her lovely day, and if it was going to be the only day they spent together in a carefree atmosphere of enjoyment she would make the most of every second. Happily she trotted along beside him as he looked for a café that appealed to him. If she hadn't still felt a tiny bit self-conscious with the man she would have danced along.

He soon found what he was looking for—an outdoor café in a small park, with tables under huge red umbrellas and trees branching all around, filtering the sunlight.

'Heaven!' Lissa murmured, sipping Pernod and Evian water from a long glass with ice tinkling in it. 'I like your Paris.'

'*My* Paris?' Hugh raised an eyebrow lazily. 'Well, yes, I suppose I can lay a half-claim to it, although I've never actually lived in France. My mother made sure I was bilingual as I grew up. I think she always hoped to bring me back here—but it wasn't to be.'

'You took over the business in England when your father died?' Lissa prompted. She wanted to know all about him, every little detail. It seemed unbelievable that she knew hardly anything.

Hugh was drinking Pernod too. He took a long swig of it before he replied, sitting back and looking up into the trees thoughtfully. 'I took over the business quite a while *before* my father died. Before my mother divorced him, as a matter of fact. I'd been working with him ever since I left university, and eventually it became obvious that he wasn't pulling his weight—he had what is euphemistically known as a drink problem.' He smiled grimly.

'After the divorce things got worse and I was running the business single-handed. I suppose I enjoyed it—I could get things going my own way and he really wasn't very interested. Then he married again and for a few months he seemed to be improving, but it didn't last. He died just over two years ago. My stepmother had her own private income and he left me three quarters of the business and the other quarter to my stepmother's son—Paul Donaldson, whom I believe you know.' He cast her a mocking glance.

For a moment a shadow seemed to fall across the sunlit grass. Lissa said, 'Don't let's bring all that up again—not now—*please*.'

At the urgency in her voice he gave her a not-very-pleasant smile. 'Missing him, are you?'

'I just don't want to spoil our day by—by niggling,' she said in a rather choked voice.

He nodded slowly. 'You must forgive me. I'm like the patient who keeps on taking his temperature to see if he's better.'

There was only one construction she could put on that. She put down her glass with a thud. 'Aren't you satisfied with the work I'm doing, then? Are you accusing me of—of wasting my time dreaming about Paul?'

He stretched across the table and covered her hand with his. 'Calm down, sweetheart, I'm not accusing you of anything and your work is entirely satisfactory. Excellent, in fact.' He held on to her hand and smiled at her, the rare smile that made her heart lurch in her breast. 'No more niggling, I promise. And we'll have a good day. Now, if you've finished, shall we make a start?'

It was more than a good day, it was pure magic. The sun never went in for a moment, and even if it had done Lissa was sure she wouldn't have noticed. Hugh was beside her and that made everything perfect.

The crush of people in the Louvre meant that his arm was round her, guiding her between the tangle of visitors to peer round bodies at the famous paintings she had picked out to see, chief among which was the *Mona Lisa*. She gazed at it for a long time, bemused and speechless, and at last whispered, 'Let's go now.'

'You're OK?' Hugh asked when they were outside again.

She nodded. 'A bit overcome, that's all. You see so many photographs and prints of a great masterpiece like that and then, suddenly, there's the real thing and it's quite, quite different. It—sort of—made me feel rather strange.'

Hugh was looking at her oddly. 'I was going to suggest Notre Dame next but maybe that will have an equally unsettling effect.'

'You're making fun of me,' she accused.

'Never! I'm learning all the time,' he said lightly. 'Come along, we'll risk Notre Dame.'

There was a service in progress but the congregation seemed to be swallowed up in the dim, chilly, inner recesses of the great Gothic cathedral. It seemed that the tourists in the outer aisles outnumbered them, some in couples, some in groups with their guides, and there was a constant rustle of guidebooks and the sound of hushed commentaries. Lissa drew Hugh away into a corner, catching her breath with wonder at the soaring height of the ancient building, at the massive pillars, at the great rose-window that seemed to float in the darkness like a giant jewel.

The mass was nearing its climax. The priest's voice echoed through the vast space inside the cathedral. Lissa gripped Hugh's arm, watching with a feeling of awe. And then the spell was broken. As the white-surpliced priest held the host high in his hands, facing the congregation, there was a clicking and flashing of dozens of cameras from the outer aisles.

'Oh,' gasped Lissa. 'They shouldn't . . .'

Hugh was watching her expression. 'We go?' he questioned, and she nodded.

Outside, they walked through the gardens. 'What was it this time?' he teased. 'You had that same look on your face.'

'What look?' Lissa asked.

'A look I'm beginning to recognise,' he said. 'When I've pinned it down I'll let you know. Now, we really will put something lighter on the menu, but almost equally huge in its conception. Except that it's twentieth century, not thirteenth.'

'Let me guess—the Pompidou Centre?'

'Clever girl.' He linked his arm through hers. 'The "in" place at the moment is the Musée d'Orsay, where all the great Impressionists are on show now. But we might have to queue there, so we'll give it a miss. On to the Pompidou—anyway, it's more fun.'

After that the whole day turned into pure fun. At the Pompidou Centre they rode in escalators in plastic tubes that clung to the side of the extraordinary building. They gazed down at the groups of entertainers in the piazza below. They wandered through galleries of art and sculpture—huge, airy rooms, everything modern and expertly planned.

'Fantastic, isn't it?' Hugh enthused as they sat having a cafeteria lunch on the roof terrace. 'The technology that's gone into this building is quite staggering.'

'What about the technology that must have gone into the building of Notre Dame?' Lissa retorted.

'And they didn't have computers to do all the planning for them in those days.'

Hugh grinned at her. 'Do I detect a note of criticism? I thought you were a girl with her eyes on the future?'

'The future comes from the present and the present from the past, surely?' Lissa felt confident enough to argue with him now. 'Cause and effect. That's logic.' She cast a mischievous glance at him.

'Touché.' His mouth turned down ruefully. 'I can see you are going to keep me on my toes, where my pet hobby-horse is concerned. After lunch we shall tackle the Faubourg-St-Honoré, and you can gaze with feminine delight on the elegant gowns, and a mere man won't feel the need to express an opinion.'

The golden hours passed almost in a dream. They laughed and argued together and walked hand in hand like lovers. Hugh observed that touring Paris meant spending most of the time on foot, so the little cafés that popped up everywhere were a godsend. But, even allowing for stops en route, most of Lissa's itinerary was covered and at last, rather weary, they ended up sitting on the quayside, lazily watching the pavement artists and the customers at the little bookshops, and the small craft that moved busily along the river in the hazy sunlight of late afternoon.

'A river trip would have rounded out the sightseeing,' Hugh observed. 'We might do that another day.'

Did he really mean that, or was he merely being polite? Lissa let out her breath on a long sigh. 'Oh, it's been wonderful. My first sight of Paris and it couldn't have been better. I'm really grateful.'

'I'm grateful too,' he said, stretching out his long legs before him. 'I've learned a lot today.'

'*You've* learned a lot? I'd have thought you knew Paris by heart.'

He turned his head and in the shadow of the trees his eyes were dark and liquid like the grey of the river. 'Ah, but I wasn't talking about Paris,' he said softly.

Lissa looked up, startled, and then found she couldn't look away again. His eyes held hers and she was sinking, drowning in a deep, deep sea.

She shook her head, passing her tongue over her dry lips, saying the first thing that came into her head. 'Do you think—is there anywhere to get a drink here? Water would do—I'm really thirsty.'

'Of course—we passed a kiosk selling ice-cream a little way back. Wait here and I'll bring you some. And I can promise it won't be like any other ice-cream you've ever tasted.'

As the first delicious spoonful slid down Lissa's parched throat she crooned with delight. The creaminess, the velvety smoothness, the sweet, subtle flavour! 'Good?' Hugh enquired with a sideways grin, as he applied himself to his own tub. 'I told you so.'

'Um—heaven,' Lissa sighed dreamily. She scraped up the last melting blob greedily. 'I didn't know ice-cream could taste like this.'

'Ice-cream is something we do rather well in France,' Hugh said, looking hard at her. 'You've left a bit at the side of your mouth. Allow me.' He leant over and licked off the melting drops.

'Delicious,' he murmured, and his tongue moved to trace the softness of her lips and then, for a second, ventured between them.

It was merely a quick, playful kiss, but Lissa's head swam with delight. Hugh moved away and sighed. 'A shame we have to make a move, but Maman will be expecting us home for dinner.'

He's enjoyed the day, Lissa thought. Sitting here with Hugh beside her she seemed to be drowning in happiness. He hadn't really wanted to come but he'd enjoyed himself after all. Perhaps he really did mean to bring her here again. That seemed to add the final touch of pleasure to the day.

'And I've got a good deal of back-work to make up this evening,' he added, getting to his feet. 'A day off has to be made up.'

'Yes, of course.' Lissa agreed in a small voice. Oh, why did he have to say that? Why couldn't he have let me have my dream-day without bringing me back to reality at the very end?

She glanced at his suddenly preoccupied face. He had done his duty, he had rewarded her for being an obedient guinea-pig and now he could get on with his real interest in life. She supposed she should have expected it, but it sent her down into a black pit of despair just the same.

CHAPTER SIX

HUGH took the plastic ice-cream tubs and spoons and dropped them in a waste receptacle. Then he came back and said, 'We ought to call in at Claude's gallery while we're in town, just to see how he's getting on. He's bound to be working late, his new exhibition opens on Saturday.'

This time there was no lingering in the dark caverns of the car park; Hugh was anxious to be on his way. 'We'll go by way of the gallery—it's off the Boulevard-St-Germain,' he announced as the car wove its way up into the daylight. 'If there's a parking space anywhere near we'll pop in for a few minutes. If not we'll go straight home.'

Lissa didn't agree or disagree; she hadn't been asked. She hoped fervently that there wouldn't be a parking space because it seemed likely that Carolyn would be at the gallery, and the prospect of meeting the girl again made her feel distinctly uneasy.

As for Hugh—all the lazy, relaxed friendliness of the day had gone. He was his usual crisp, businesslike self again as he eased the Renault into a parking space a short time later. Of course, Lissa thought glumly, there *would* be a parking space. Her luck had run out.

She hurried after Hugh along a narrow street where the shops looked fascinating—bookshops, antique shops, shops with maps and prints in the

window, some with trendy, colourful clothes. The
shops were still open but there was no time to stop
and browse—Hugh had already reached the gallery
and was knocking at the closed door beside the great
plate-glass window, with 'Galerie Delage' splashed
across it in gold lettering.

Claude himself opened the door and greeted them
with delighted surprise. He was in shirt-sleeves, his
sleek dark hair slightly ruffled, his quizzical black
eyes glowing with almost childish glee. 'You come
to see our—how do you say—muddle? We are indeed up to our eyes.' He beamed at Lissa, pleased
with his command of the English language, and led
the way through the front lobby into a large main
gallery, where framed pictures were propped on the
floor at intervals, their faces to the bare white walls.

A table stood in the centre of the room, filled
with catalogues, invitation cards, sheets of stick-on
numbers, glossy international art magazines. A
young man, wearing a multi-coloured designer
sweatshirt, a Gauloise hanging from the side of his
mouth, was painstakingly typing labels. Claude introduced him as Philippe and he stood up and
bowed politely, casting frankly interested looks at
Lissa.

'We work hard and it is very hot.' Claude fanned
himself with his hand. 'But we must 'ave everything ready for our *vernissage*—our private view.
The small gallery is ready for hanging tomorrow.
You see?' He led the way through an arch into a
smaller gallery beyond.

Lissa's heart sank. Carolyn, in bright pink jeans
and smock, was sitting on top of a ladder apatheti-

cally filling in some tiny holes in the wall with plaster and a palette knife.

'Hughie! I knew it was your voice.' She slithered down the ladder, dropped the knife, and ran to Hugh's side, clutching his arm. 'Darling, darling Hugh, you must help me, I can't . . .'

The rest of her words were lost to Lissa as Claude began to lead her round, turning back one or two of the pictures for her to admire, talking volubly in his slightly fractured English. She smiled and murmured and tried unsuccessfully to hear what Carolyn was saying at the far side of the room.

'Claude—*un moment, s'il te plaît*,' Hugh called and Claude, with a polite little bow of apology, joined the other two. Carolyn had her arm linked firmly with Hugh's now and her huge blue eyes were bright with tears.

Lissa wandered back into the larger gallery and picked up one of the catalogues from a stack on the table. Philippe, the young assistant at the typewriter, grinned winningly at her and burst into a torrent of French, of which she didn't understand a word. She smiled vaguely at him and walked across to the big plate-glass window, to stare blindly out into the street.

The other three returned to the room and Hugh walked across to Lissa and put an arm round her shoulder. 'Sweetheart, will you excuse me for a short time? Carolyn has a problem with her landlady and I must go along and sort it out. Claude will look after you while I'm away. OK?'

The kiss he dropped on her forehead and the deep caress in his voice as he added, 'See you soon,' were both, of course, for Carolyn's benefit. The girl hadn't acknowledged Lissa's presence, but as she left the gallery, still hanging on to Hugh's arm, she threw her a glance as full of venom as a poisoned dart.

She hasn't given up, Lissa thought. Perhaps she will get him in the end. She watched them through the window as they crossed the road together, Hugh's dark head leaning down towards the silky blonde one, Carolyn gazing up adoringly at him. And suddenly she felt tired and hot and her feet were aching and she would have liked to crawl away somewhere and weep because her lovely day was quite, quite spoiled now.

Claude had come up behind her and he, too, was watching the couple walking away—the supple pink figure dancing along beside the tall, lithe one.

'Hugh is a brilliant young man,' he murmured drily, 'but your brilliant man can be very stupid where a clever, scheming woman is concerned. *Mais alors*, Lissa, there is coffee in the office. We will drink together and await Hugh's return.'

Lissa turned and met the faintly cynical dark eyes. Carolyn—clever—scheming? That certainly wasn't how Hugh saw her. To him she was a pretty, guileless child who had grown fond of him because he had befriended her.

Which was true? As Lissa followed the Frenchman to the office she remembered the look of sheer hate that Carolyn had directed at her, and thought she knew.

An hour passed and Hugh had not come back. Lissa had drunk several cups of coffee which she didn't want and pretended to read several art magazines which she couldn't understand. Her feelings were decidedly mixed: partly anger at being dumped here at Carolyn's whim, partly anxiety about what Hugh and Carolyn were doing all this time, but mostly disappointment that a day which had promised so much was ending in such a dreary, inconclusive fashion.

At seven o'clock Claude came into the office, looking tired and hot. 'We 'ave finished for today,' he said, 'and Hugh 'as not returned. I suggest we go home without him, Lissa, if you are agreeable. I am sure that a good dinner awaits us there.'

Lissa jumped to her feet immediately. 'I'm quite agreeable, Monsieur Delage. Hugh has his car, he can drive himself home when he's ready.' And if she sounded uptight that was exactly how she was feeling.

Sitting beside Claude in the smooth luxury of his big car, Lissa could have wept, thinking of how she might have been sitting beside Hugh. All her thoughts were of Hugh, she couldn't get him out of her mind for a second. To avoid the danger of making a fool of herself by bursting into tears, she chattered on about everything she had seen that day in Paris, and what a marvellous city Paris was— with which Claude agreed heartily.

When they arrived at Claude's home he switched off the engine and turned to Lissa, patting her cold hand, and said, 'Do not worry, *ma chère*, it will all be well in the end, you will see.'

He must have known how she was feeling. She was tempted to blurt out the truth. Hugh had evidently not told his parents about the stupid charade he had dreamed up, and if she tried to explain now it would only make everything more complicated.

Once in the house explanations had to be made to Madame Delage, who didn't trouble to hide her annoyance. 'It was too bad of Hugh to leave you and go off with Carolyn like that.' Her brown eyes glinted with displeasure. 'I shall tell him so when he comes in.'

'Oh, please don't,' Lissa said hastily. 'It didn't matter a bit and we had a lovely time seeing all the sights in Paris.'

Monique was looking rather hard at her and Lissa was once again alarmed that she was showing her feelings too obviously. 'It was very hot,' she said, 'and sightseeing is always a bit hard on the feet, isn't it? Shall I have time for a quick shower before dinner?'

'Of course, my dear. Dinner will probably be a little later than usual. Marie has her sister and brother-in-law and their little boy staying here with her for a couple of days on their annual holiday and Marie is all excitement, as you may imagine. We'll say half-past eight for dinner. Hugh should certainly be back by then.'

But Hugh was not back by half-past eight. In fact, dinner was over, Monsieur Delage had retired to work in his study, and Monique and Lissa were lingering over their coffee when the door opened and Hugh came in—with Carolyn hesitating behind him, looking wide-eyed and anxious.

'Maman dear, forgive us. I hope you haven't waited.' Hugh, looking suitably remorseful, came further into the room. 'And Lissa darling, I'm full of apologies for leaving you, but when you've heard the reason I'm sure you'll understand.' He put an arm round Lissa's shoulder and laid his cheek briefly against her hair.

She sat stiffly, receiving the mock-caress. He was still keeping up the stupid farce, she thought with disgust. Why bother, when it was obvious that Carolyn only had to lift her little finger to have him running to comply with her every wish?

He had gone back to take Carolyn's hand and draw her towards his mother. 'Maman, this child is feeling absurdly guilty about putting you out. The fact is that she has nowhere to rest her pretty head tonight.' He smiled indulgently at Carolyn, whose great blue eyes were misted with tears.

'She's been having a bad time with her landlady for some weeks, she tells me, and today it came to a crisis. I went with her to interview the lady and she certainly is a battleaxe. She made some quite unforgivable accusations and it was all very unpleasant. In the end the only thing was for Carolyn to pack her bags and get out. We looked around for a while but there was nowhere suitable for her to stay, so I suggested she should come back here for tonight and we'll find new digs for her tomorrow.'

Carolyn turned her huge blue eyes from Hugh to his mother. 'I feel terrible about imposing myself on you at such short notice, *madame*. I could sleep anywhere, you know. On the floor or on a sofa or anywhere.' The soft lips quivered.

Monique said briskly, 'Oh, that won't be necessary, I'm sure we can find a bed for you.' Appearing to remember her obligation as a hostess, she added, 'We're pleased to have you, Carolyn.

I'll go and fix up a room for you.' Turning to Hugh she added, 'Sit down, both of you, and I'll have some dinner sent in.'

The faint chill in her usually pleasant voice was unmistakable and Lissa saw Hugh's eyebrows lift slightly before he pulled out a chair for Carolyn at the empty place that had been set for him.

Lissa stood up. 'You can have my chair, Hugh,' she said. 'I've finished dinner.'

'Oh, but . . .' he demurred, frowning.

'I've arranged to phone my parents about now,' she said sweetly. 'They'll be waiting for a call. Please excuse me.' She went out and left them together and as she reached the door she saw, out of the corner of her eye, Carolyn lay her white hand on Hugh's sleeve and lean confidingly towards him.

In her bedroom Lissa sat on the bed and waited to get into a better frame of mind before she put the call through to Florida. The call she'd made earlier in the week had been very brief, but now she longed to hear her mother's placid, ordinary voice, to bring her back into a world where she wasn't torn apart by emotions she couldn't really understand.

'Darling, how lovely! We've been waiting for your call.' Her mother sounded so close and so comfortingly normal. 'I just can't get used to talking to you from thousands of miles away. Are you still in France and are you enjoying life and have you seen Paris?'

Lissa swallowed. 'Yes, I'm still in France and we've been to Paris today. I can't wait to tell you all about it. What have you and Daddy been up to? Have you been behaving yourselves?'

'Oh, a glorious time, darling. Absolutely out of this world. Miami Beach has to be seen to be believed, and the sun has shone all the time. We've been everywhere and done everything. Had a day at the Everglades and we actually saw an alligator. And the birds! Marvellous colours, quite unbelievable! And yesterday—you'll laugh—we went to Disneyworld. I've always been a bit sniffy about Disneyworld, haven't I? But it really is quite stupendous. We've got loads of pictures. Everything's so colossal here and everyone's on the go all the time. It'll be quite a change to get back to sleepy Streatham.'

Lissa had never heard her usually calm mother sound so excited. 'You must be having a wonderful time. I can't wait to hear all about it.' She tried not to sound gloomy. 'When are you coming back?'

'We leave for New York on Tuesday—I *had* to see New York. We'll stay the night and fly back Wednesday. Should be home Wednesday night. How about you?'

'I'm not sure yet,' Lissa said. 'It hasn't been fixed. You've got my number here, give me a ring when you get home, won't you?'

'Will do,' her mother said cheerfully. 'Look after yourself and be good. Say hello to Daddy.'

Lissa talked for another few minutes, and when she put the receiver down she consulted her watch and jotted down the time the call had taken. She was determined to pay for her calls and not be under an obligation to Hugh.

She felt better for her talk to her parents, as she'd known she would. It was like a link with an ordinary, sane world she'd been happy in before she'd fallen in love.

She sat for a long time on the bed, staring ahead of her, trying to come to terms with what had happened. Nothing in her previous experience had prepared her to handle the raw emotion that shook her every time she saw the man, even heard his voice. If it was body chemistry, then it must be like one of those mysterious substances marked 'DANGER' which were kept underwater in glass bottles in the lab at school, and which burst into flame if—against all the rules—you took the stopper off.

She had always thought of herself as a modern, reasonably level-headed girl. She'd never had the urge to mix with a really outrageous set, either at school or later. There had never been any shortage of dates, but she'd always been careful to avoid any serious commitment. And—except for one incident in her student days which she preferred to forget—if her dates expected more than a goodnight kiss they were disappointed.

A nice, ordinary, quite pretty, not very exciting girl with a job she enjoyed, living at home with her parents in a suburban house, playing tennis and badminton, joining in amateur theatricals in the winter. That was how she'd seen herself. One day, she had thought, she would fall in love and marry, have children and settle down to a life very similar to her parents' life.

She hadn't reckoned on falling in love being such an overwhelming event, taking you over and mixing all your emotions into a seething, bubbling witch's brew, putting a spell on you which turned you into a different person. She thought of Hugh and

Carolyn sitting close together at the dinner table and a shaft of pain cut through her so sharp and keen that she had to lean forward, clasping her arms round her body.

A knock at the door made her jump up, and when Hugh came into the room she goggled at him as if some terrifying phantom of her imagination had just materialised.

He walked over to her, dark brows raised. 'What's wrong, Lissa? You look as if you'd seen a ghost.'

She passed her tongue over her dry lips. 'I was thinking. You startled me.'

'I came to see what had happened to you—you were so long away. I thought I might be able to help you if you couldn't get your call through to your parents.'

'Thank you,' she said stiffly. 'I managed perfectly well—you needn't have left Carolyn. And by the way,' she found the courage to go on, 'don't you think we might put an end to this imaginary affair between us? There really isn't any point in it. Never was, really.'

A gleam came into the silver-grey eyes. 'Well, well, you wouldn't by any chance be jealous, would you, Lissa?'

'Jealous?' she squeaked. 'How ridiculous! I merely wondered why you needed me to protect you from your friend Carolyn when you're so obviously willing to jump to do her bidding. I'm quite sure she's not convinced that you have the least interest in me.'

'Think so? Well, then, we'll have to make it more convincing, won't we?'

There was a dangerous glint in his eyes that sent a shiver spiralling through Lissa's body and when he came nearer she backed away until she was standing up against the wall beside the bed.

'Won't we?' he said again, very softly. 'Perhaps a little practice would help.'

As his arms closed round her she murmured, 'No—you mustn't—I can't,' but her hands went up—seemingly of their own accord—to bury themselves in the soft hair at the back of his neck.

'I haven't kissed you properly yet,' Hugh said. 'Perhaps that's what's wrong.'

Dimly she knew that he was a long way from being carried away by passion, while she was dangerously close. She looked into his eyes, and their silvery greyness was like a calm lake. His lips were curved in a whimsical smile that seemed to mock the tumult that was rushing through her. She fastened her gaze on his mouth and a wave of longing swept over her. If he didn't kiss her she would faint—she would die, she thought light-headedly.

'I'll demonstrate, shall I?' he murmured against her lips and then his mouth fastened on hers and the dream became reality. She closed her eyes and revelled in the sensations he was arousing in her as his lips traced the shape of her mouth, then travelled down to bury themselves sensuously in the hollow of her neck, then returned to tease her own lips apart and explore the depths within.

She was so near the bed that it took only a gentle pressure of his hands on her back to ease her down so that she was lying full-length, looking up into

Hugh's face as he lay beside her, propped up on one elbow.

'You're beautiful,' he breathed softly. 'So beautiful. What I could do to you, Lissa! Would you like to find out? Would you like me to show you?'

Her head was spinning. She felt dizzy and weak and she was almost out of control. Almost. But somewhere at the back of her mind she registered the fact that Hugh was very much *in* control of the proceedings. She bit her lip hard and shook her head and the tawny curls foamed out over the pillow.

His fingers thrust into the mass of hair, tumbling it, tugging at it. Then, quite suddenly, she felt him change. She recognised the exact moment when he wasn't flirting any longer, when he was taken over by a savage, elemental need. He flung one leg across her body, pressing against her, making her aware of his arousal, sending a fierce thrill spiralling through her.

There was no question of Lissa resisting. She had fallen in love with him from the first moment they'd met, and this was the inevitable result.

She heard him groan, 'Oh, well, why did I have to *ask* you?' He drew in a long, uneven breath and she felt his whole body move in a deep shudder. His hand was on her blouse, wrenching open the buttons, feeling its way inside to close over the thin gossamer of her bra.

'Can't you undo this thing?' he muttered, and, as his fingers touched the hardened peak thrusting against the delicate material, a jolt of pure ecstasy rocked through her, making her whimper for more—more——

His hand slipped under the elasticated belt of her skirt, and was working its way downwards, while Lissa held her breath, waiting for what she was sure would come next.

Then, through the tumult that was pulsing through her, she suddenly realised that Hugh had rolled away from her and was sitting on the edge of the bed, his back to her, his head in his hands, and that he was swearing colourfully. She also realised that loud noises were coming from the office-room next door—banging and thudding and clattering.

'Bloody bad timing!' Hugh muttered. He turned and flung himself into the cane chair near the bed and sat glowering down at his feet.

Lissa pulled herself up in the bed, her fingers shaking as she fastened the buttons of her blouse. 'What's—what's going on in there?'

'I'd say at a guess that it's Marie and all her damned family putting up a camp-bed,' he growled disgustedly.

'For Carolyn?' That was all that Lissa could think of.

'No, for me. Carolyn is to have my room—the room I've been sleeping in upstairs. That's my mother's idea.' He frowned darkly. 'I feel like the loser in a game of musical chairs. Only it's musical bedrooms.'

'You're going to sleep in—in there?' Lissa said faintly. Oh, lord, she thought—away from the rest of the house and with only a door between them!

'That's what I said.' He bit out the words savagely. 'Maman probably thinks she's doing us a good turn.'

Having said which he fell into a brooding silence, kicking at the thick cream carpet with the heel of his shoe.

After a full minute of that Lissa felt like screaming. 'Stop it,' she said sharply.

He gave her a look of pure amazement and stopped kicking. 'Lissa,' he said huskily. 'We must talk.'

Suddenly she had a curious certainty that she was more in control of this situation than he was. 'Yes?' she said coolly. She pulled her knees up and wrapped her arms round them, gazing at him innocently. 'I'm sitting comfortably, so you can begin.'

'This isn't funny,' he growled. 'It puts me in a spot.'

'I don't see why. If you don't think you'll be comfortable on a camp-bed you can have your own room back and I'll sleep in there.'

She saw his hands clench until the knuckles showed white, and knew she was getting under his skin. 'Don't pretend to be naïve,' he ground out. 'You're not a child, Lissa. No girl who's been dating my stepbrother Paul could be an innocent.'

Lissa's green eyes flared and she very nearly came back at him with a furious denial. But what was the use? He hadn't believed her when she had denied it before, why should he do so now? And anyway, she thought, it might be better to let him think she was in love with Paul. It would act as a kind of shield against letting herself get completely carried away if Hugh had any idea of repeating what he'd called his 'demonstration'.

So she shrugged and said nothing.

The silver-grey eyes fixed themselves on her feet and then moved upwards towards her knees. Lissa had a panicky feeling that she hadn't pulled her skirt down far enough, but she was totally unable to move. His gaze travelled slowly upwards resting with unconcealed interest on her breasts, where the nipples were straining against her thin blouse, and finally coming to rest on her own eyes that stared, half-hypnotised, into his.

'Oh, *hell*!' he burst out in furious exasperation, jumping to his feet and beginning to stride up and down the room. Lissa watched him in silence. It was like watching a kettle come to the boil and blow off its lid. Slowly the pressure subsided and he stopped walking and sat down again.

He faced her seriously. 'We've got a problem, Lissa, and the only thing to do with a problem is to think it through reasonably.' Ah, yes, she thought, the momentary madness was over. Hugh was himself again—resolute, logical, hard as nails. 'The fact is that—like it or not—I find you extremely attractive and, to put it bluntly, I very much want to make love to you. It's a fact that I hadn't counted on when I suggested your coming here, but it's a fact that must be faced and dealt with now.'

His eyes, meeting hers, were cool and detached. Such a short time before he had been trembling with passion, generating a heat that had almost scorched her, and now he had switched over to this other side of himself, the logical, reasonable side, which he no doubt preferred. What an incredible man!

'I don't see any problem,' she said coldly. The chill had reached her—it was like opening the lid of a freezer. Very soon she would be a solid block of ice herself. 'I would hate to be any sort of an embarrassment to you. I suggest that I go back to England immediately.'

'No,' he shot out, and then, seeming to remember that he was being cool and reasonable, went on, 'No, that wouldn't do. I need you here until you've finished the work on the manual. I reckon another three or four days should complete the job. I can't let you go until Wednesday at the earliest. You've really done extremely well up to now, but you've still got to tackle the spreadsheet—which may produce some tricky problems.'

'The problem still remains, though; if I'm around you might run the danger of losing your cool again?' Lissa said, her lip twisting.

He shot her a suspicious glance. 'Precisely,' he said crisply. 'I happen to be a man.'

'And I happen to be a woman. Inconvenient, isn't it?'

'I'm not so sure. It might just work out advantageous to both of us. You know my attitude towards any permanent commitment. I know you're still carrying a torch for Paul. But I also know that you want me as much as I want you. OK, so we won't romanticise it. It's simply a healthy physical reaction. So why deny it? We'd both work better if we weren't continually frustrated.'

Lissa stared at him in a fascinated way—as she might have stared at a dangerous wild animal. She said very quietly, 'What exactly are you suggesting? One night? Two nights? Three? Or would it be one of your—what did you call it?—your long-term commitments with no strings on either side?'

'It's up to you, Lissa.' Incredulous, she saw that he had taken her words entirely at their face value. 'Whatever you say. You could rely on me to be absolutely reasonable about—about everything.'

She was choking with anger now. She wanted to hit out at him, to wipe that self-satisfied smile off his lips. But if she let go and screamed at him it would get her nowhere—and, worst of all, he wouldn't have the faintest idea why she was so upset. There was only one way to deal with him and that was to play the game according to his rules.

She drew in a quick breath. 'There's really nothing to say except——' she met his eyes steadily '—except no. No, no, *no*.'

She saw him go pale and felt a small sense of triumph. He hadn't expected that, had he?

'All right,' he said coldly. 'I heard you the first time. No need to repeat yourself. And I think this conversation has gone on long enough. I'd better see what's happening next door.'

'Wait a minute.' Lissa swung her legs off the bed and stood up. Her knees were shaky, but the emotional chaos inside her was subsiding, leaving her feeling empty and exhausted.

She eyed him levelly. 'I'd like to get my situation here absolutely clear. You said three or four days to complete my work on the manual. I'd be glad if you'd make arrangements for me to leave on Wednesday. My parents will be back from Florida by then, so I shan't have any problem about going home. As regards my job, I'll send in my notice when I get back.'

'You want to leave the company? Give up your job?' His amazement was genuine. 'Why, for goodness' sake? You've more than proved your capabilities in the work you've been doing here; it's clear that you've got a very good brain for technology and with further training you could make your way up the ladder on the technical side of the business. If you're tired of office work you might transfer to our factory in Dorset. You'd like it there—it's situated in a very pleasant spot.'

She said coolly, 'Do you work there yourself?'

Again he looked faintly puzzled. 'I come and go.' Then his face cleared and his mouth set in a cynical line. 'Oh, I see. Well, I shouldn't embarrass you with any more of my—unwelcome advances, if that's what's bothering you.'

She winced inside with pain. What had happened to their easy friendship of this afternoon? He had been so human, such fun to be with, and now he had turned into an ice-man. She felt scalding tears gathering behind her eyelids, but whatever happened he mustn't see her cry.

She turned away and went across to the dressing-table to pick up a brush. 'I'll think about it,' she said briefly, and began to brush her hair into something like tidiness. In the mirror she saw him hesitate for a moment, then he shrugged and went out through the connecting door into the office.

He reappeared in the doorway a moment later. 'They've gone,' he said. 'I suppose I should thank them for saving me from making a fool of myself.' He looked down at the door. 'There isn't a lock. I would suggest you put up a barricade if you feel yourself threatened.'

She hated the bitterness in his voice. He was a proud man and she had rejected him—that must hurt, whatever the particular circumstances.

She went across and stood in front of him—not too near. 'Hugh,' she said, 'I'm sorry for my part in all this. I shouldn't have let you——' her voice faltered, but she plucked up her courage and went on '—let you go so far. You're not the only one who feels frustrated, you know.'

A gleam came into his grey eyes. 'Then why not...?'

But she shook her head. 'Sex for its own sake may be good enough for you, but it's not good enough for me. There has to be something more.'

'What is known as love?' he sneered, sitting in a nearby chair. 'That fiction kept going by your sex, in the face of all the divorce statistics?'

She met the mockery in the cold grey eyes without flinching. 'Yes, I mean love, and if you don't know what I'm talking about then I'm sorry for you.'

'Oh, I know what you're talking about. And I also know what love does to you—it blinds you to reason and common sense. And I don't want to be blinded. It may be selfish, but that's the way I am.'

'Poor Hugh,' she said. 'I feel so sorry for you.'

He got to his feet. 'You can cut out the irony,' he said harshly. 'I've told you how I'm made and it's no good trying to make me feel guilty about it. Now, shall we go back and show our faces before they all begin to wonder what we're getting up to? We've been away long enough for Carolyn to get the message.'

So that was the reason why he had come to look for her! 'Must we still keep up that stupid charade?'

she said shortly. The thought of pretending to be having an affair with Hugh had suddenly become almost unbearable.

'Oh, yes, it's working like a charm. I do believe Carolyn is beginning to recognise the fact that she can't make me into husband material. Come along.' He stood waiting for her by the door, tall and fabulously good-looking and completely in control of himself—a maddening, cynical, fascinating, seductive—*monster*.

'Oh, and by the way, you needn't put up a barricade tonight.' He looked down at her with a twisted smile as she joined him. 'You've managed very effectively to put my—er—ardour into cold storage.'

Lissa walked through the doorway before him, keeping as far away as possible. For the moment her own feelings were in cold storage too, but if she touched him—even if she brushed against him— she would melt into his arms and agree to anything he suggested. A little time in paradise and then years of regret and black misery!

No, she thought, holding her head high as she preceded him into the salon, it's not a fair exchange and I won't let it happen. But the night ahead, with only an unlocked door between them, was going to be a stern test.

Carolyn was alone in the salon. She jumped up as soon as she saw Hugh and ran across to him. 'Hughie, I've brought your coffee in, you didn't finish it.' She took his hand to lead him over to the table, but he gently disengaged himself.

'Thanks, Carolyn, but I've had all the coffee I want.'

'Well, come and sit down and talk to me, then,' she urged prettily.

'Sorry, sweetheart, I've got work to do.' He was so kind to her, so gentle, it made Lissa's blood boil. 'I'll probably be working late but I'll see you in the morning and we can arrange about finding new digs for you.' He patted her smooth white-gold hair. 'Sleep well.'

Lissa had walked to the far side of the room and was pretending to admire a polished brass plant-holder on a side-table.

Hugh cast an overtly intimate look at her. 'See you later, Lissa darling,' he murmured as he went out of the room.

What was she supposed to do? she thought furiously. Throw him a knowing, inviting glance? She'd rather have thrown the brass plant-holder at him. Well, at least she didn't have to stay here and carry on the farce with Carolyn. She turned towards the door.

But the girl was there before her. Her blue eyes were hard as marbles. She thrust her face towards Lissa and the cheekbones were stained with ugly colour. 'I suppose you think he'll marry you, do you? He won't, you know. I don't care if he has his dolly-girls to give him sex for what they can get out of it.' Her voice was peevish, her mouth sulky. 'He'll come back to me when he's tired of you—he always does. I only have to ask and he does anything I want. He loves me—I know he does—I know—he'll marry me in the end.' The voice rose shrilly.

Lissa regarded the weak, pretty face with distaste. 'I wouldn't bet on it,' she said. 'Now, if you'll excuse me...' She swept past Carolyn, leaving the girl staring stupidly after her.

Crossing the hall to her room she met Monique coming downstairs, looking quite put out. 'What a nuisance!' She wrinkled her nose. 'Marie isn't too pleased about having to move the rooms around again. Such a pity this happened when we've got a houseful. Still, she's coping. Where is everyone?'

'Carolyn's in the salon,' Lissa told her. 'Hugh's gone to his office to work—and he wants me to help him.' That little white lie wouldn't hurt anyone and nothing would persuade her to spend the rest of the evening in Carolyn's company.

Monique sighed and pulled a face. 'Oh, well, I suppose I'd better go and do my duty as a hostess. Goodnight, my dear. Don't let my son work you too hard.' She smiled suddenly and leaned forward and kissed Lissa's cheek before she went on into the salon.

Lissa walked across the hall. It was hateful to have to deceive Hugh's mother, especially when she seemed to approve of what she imagined was her son's choice of a girlfriend.

In her bedroom Lissa switched on the bedside lamp, drew up a chair and settled herself down to read. There was no sound from the office next door, but she had a clear picture in her mind of Hugh sitting at his desk, pen in hand, a frown of concentration on his face as he jotted down details on a pad, with many crossings-out and fresh starts. She wondered what he was doing now that was so important. So far as she knew he had finished work on the manual—keeping one step in front of her all the time.

Perhaps he wasn't working at all, perhaps that had just been an excuse to get away from her, and possibly from Carolyn too. Perhaps he wasn't in the office at all. There was a side-door into the garden and he could have gone out—driven into Paris. She wished she knew where he was. She looked nervously towards the communicating door and wondered whether she should barricade it as he'd suggested at first, or whether her refusal to fall in with his wishes had really cooled his ardour, as he had ironically told her.

An hour dragged by and Lissa had read one chapter of her book twice through, and even then hadn't taken in a word. She glanced at her watch. Ten-fifteen. By now she was quite sure that Hugh wasn't in the next room. The best thing to do was to take him at his word, go to bed and to sleep and forget all about the day's happenings. Congratulating herself that she could, at a pinch, be nearly as reasonable as Hugh himself, she undressed and washed and settled down in bed.

Another hour's unsatisfactory attempt to read the mystery story found her with heavy eyelids and no progress at all towards finding out who had done the murder. She sighed deeply, switched out the light and very quickly fell into an uneasy sleep— the kind of sleep that starts immediately with a half-waking dream.

Hugh seemed to be calling her. 'Lissa—Lissa...' She opened her mouth to call back but no sound would come past her dry, scratchy throat. Her eyes stared into the darkness. Then she saw it—the *thing* standing beside her bed, huge and black and terrifying.

She wasn't dreaming, she knew she was awake, but the *thing* was still there. Her hand went out, shaking, fumbling, to grope for the lamp-switch. Quickly—quickly—she must have light—if she had light the nameless horror would dissolve into nothing—it always did. Her finger found the switch and soft light flooded the room.

Then she froze in terror. *It* was still there, looming over her. She heard a scream. Her hands went up before her face, the room closed in on her, and with a choking sound she fell back into blackness.

CHAPTER SEVEN

LISSA opened her eyes. The room was flooded with light and she was lying on the bed with Hugh leaning over her, pushing her hair gently back off her face.

She blinked up at him stupidly. 'Wh-what happened? I remember...' She tried to sit up.

'Shush, love.' He moved a little so that he could sit beside her, one arm cradling her close to him. 'You had a fright but it's over now. You're quite safe.'

She cuddled against him, revelling in the warmth of his body through his thin shirt, the clean, male smell of him. 'Poor little girl—you had a bad dream.' His voice was so tender, so soothing as he stroked her cheek with firm fingers. She hadn't imagined Hugh could be protective like this. With Carolyn perhaps, but not with her.

'What happened?' he asked. 'A nightmare, was it?'

'Sort of.' She didn't lift her head from where it rested against his chest. She could hear the steady beat of his heart and her own heartbeat, rapid and jerky. She drew in an uneven breath. 'I've had the same one for years, only it isn't really a nightmare. I wake up and I *know* I'm awake and I see a dark, shadowy figure standing beside the bed looking at me and I'm quite paralysed with terror. I feel menaced—threatened. I try to scream but the sound won't come. I switch on the light and the figure seems to dissolve slowly. After a while I can get myself together. But this time——' She shuddered violently.

'This time you turned on the light and it didn't dissolve, it stayed there, was that it?'

'Yes,' she said in a very small voice. 'That was it. There was something there that shouldn't have been there and I couldn't make it go away.' She clung to him, reliving the terror.

She knew he was smiling, although she couldn't see his face. 'This time it was me, and I didn't go away. Poor little Lissa—I do apologise for being part of your waking nightmare.'

Her fear began to abate, her heartbeat slowed. It was heaven sitting here with Hugh's arm holding her close and Hugh being gentle and sympathetic. She wanted to stay like this for a long time, but it wasn't going to lead anywhere. She drew away and pushed back her hair, smiling shakily. 'Lissa is herself again,' she declared. 'Thanks for putting up with me.'

'My pleasure,' he said, giving her a friendly squeeze. And suddenly they were back on the amicable footing they had shared in Paris—could it be only this afternoon? It seemed weeks ago.

He slid off the bed and stood up. 'I haven't told you why I was here, scaring the wits out of you. The fact is I've been working for hours on the last section of the manual but I'm not altogether satisfied with it. I thought you might vet it for me if you were still awake. I knocked at the door and called to you and I heard an odd sort of noise. So

I came in and I was just going to switch on the light when you saw what you thought was a spook.'

So that was why he had come into her bedroom. Just for a second she had wondered... But of course, it was a business matter only.

'Sorry again,' she said. 'And to make up for the histrionics I'll gladly come and help if I can.'

'Fine. You're sure you feel equal to it? Meeting spooks in the dead of the night can take it out of you,' he said solemnly.

'Some spook! OK, I'll be with you in a minute or two.' She could feel his eyes on her bare arms and the deep cleavage of her nightdress.

He nodded. 'Cover up, won't you, or we shan't get any work done.' He didn't really mean that, of course. Work would come first.

'Of course we shall. Remember, I'm Mrs Smith when I'm in your office—a nice, fortyish lady with a husband and a son, so we won't have any funny business *if* you please.'

He didn't laugh. He said, 'I'll try very hard to remember,' and turned away abruptly and went out of the room.

Hastily, Lissa swilled her face, pulled on jeans and a sweater and joined Hugh in the office.

'Right,' he said in a businesslike tone, 'sit down and listen.' He ripped out a page from his notebook and handed it to her. 'It's the section on the spreadsheet—and don't ask me what a spreadsheet is, because nobody has yet managed to define one. All I can tell you is that there isn't much that a spreadsheet can't do. And Mrs Smith will certainly find one useful because she'll want to take all sorts of orders from different customers for her gourmet foods and she'll need to cost all the separate items frequently, as the prices change, to make sure that every job is profitable. See?'

Lissa nodded. 'Yes, I think so.'

'The difficulty,' Hugh went on, grey eyes absorbed, 'is that a micro—any micro—will eventually run out of memory. Now, there are several ways of getting round this...'

Lissa could feel her attention wavering as she looked into the depths of those keen eyes and knew that they weren't seeing her as a girl he had said he wanted to make love to. He was seeing her as Mrs Smith, a middle-aged lady who was having difficulty over a thing called a spreadsheet. I wonder if she's having difficulty over a middle-aged spread as well, Lissa thought, and had a terrible job to stop herself giggling at the feeble joke. Pull yourself together, you idiot, and listen, she told herself sternly.

Two hours later the mysteries of the spreadsheet had been more or less solved. Hugh was exultant and Lissa's cheeks were pink with the long effort of concentration.

'Splendid!' He slapped the notebook shut and dropped it on the desk. 'You're a wonder, Lissa.'

'Mrs Smith,' she reminded him, yawning.

He got up and came across to her, where she sat in front of the micro. 'Not Mrs Smith now,' he said softly. 'Lissa Stephens, a very bright young lady.'

He laid an arm round her shoulders and she felt herself melting. It took a great deal of control not to let herself lean back against him, look up into his eyes and let him see what she felt—how desperately she yearned for him. He said slowly, 'I'm not sure how I'm going to get along without you, Lissa. I've never met anyone I work so well with. Our minds seem to run along the same track.'

Our *minds*!

'How nice!' she said brightly. She stood up, disengaging herself from his hand. 'Well, if you've finished with me for the time being I think I'll go and get some sleep. I promise not to repeat my nightmare act.'

'And I promise not to appear beside your bed.' He paused. 'Unless——' his voice was suddenly hopeful '—unless you've changed your mind about my proposition.'

'I don't change my mind as easily as that,' she said, making her voice light. 'That's one track our minds don't run along together.'

He nodded briefly. 'I just thought I'd try again. But if you won't share a bed with me, at least share a nightcap.' He moved across to the cupboard where he kept a small selection of drinks.

Lissa's throat was dry and her skin was hot, which might have been the result of two hours of concentrated work—or of the sight of Hugh as he leaned down at the cupboard, dark hair rumpled, shirt hanging awry at the neck. There was something dangerously intimate about working together into the small hours in this quiet room lit only by the desk lamps over their respective work-stations. She could go over to him, put her arms round him, her fingers on the buttons of his shirt—she felt a sudden quiver between her thighs. *No,* she screamed inwardly. No, I won't be used like a—like a——

He was looking over at her questioningly, holding

two bottles aloft. 'Oh—er—just Perrier, please,' she said hastily.

'I don't call that a nightcap.' He handed her a glass. 'Just a dash of something more interesting to help you sleep. Besides, we have something to celebrate.' He held up his own glass. 'To the taming of the spreadsheet.'

'Of course, the spreadsheet.' Lissa drank the Perrier, laced with whisky, in one gulp. 'I'm glad I got the hang of it at last,' she added woodenly. 'I'll do some work on it next, just to make sure. Thanks for the drink, and I'll say goodnight now.' She stood up. 'I'll see you in the morning.'

He walked to the door with her, holding it open as she went through. 'Those words,' he said wryly, 'are the saddest I've ever heard. Goodnight, Lissa.'

She leaned back against the closed door, her eyes brimming with tears. Was she being wise—or merely prudish—or just plain stupid? She didn't know. She only knew that she was more desperately unhappy than she had ever been in her life.

Lissa had a broken, unsatisfactory night, with very little sleep, and came in to breakfast next morning feeling like death.

Monique was presiding over the enormous silver coffee-pot, Hugh sitting beside her, looking disgustingly wide awake and pleased with life.

Claude had evidently finished breakfast and was halfway to the door. 'Come along, Carolyn, *allonsy*, we must leave immediately. Good morning, Lissa, we shall see you and Hugh at our *vernissage* this evening, yes?'

He didn't wait for an answer, he was busy urging a sulky-looking Carolyn out of the room, and in another minute there was the sound of his car starting up and being driven at breakneck speed down the drive.

Monique smiled fondly. 'Claude is always like this at the beginning of an exhibition,' she explained, as Lissa took her seat at the table. 'And there is still some hanging left to do, he tells me. But I'm sure it will be "all right on the night"—it always is.'

She poured coffee and Hugh passed the cup across the table to Lissa. 'Thank you,' she murmured, not meeting his eyes, as shy as if all the fantasies that had intruded into her wakeful night had been realities. As if he had shared the big bed with her and they had made love all night long.

'Hugh tells me he kept you up late working, Lissa.' Monique sipped her coffee, looking from Lissa to her son and back again, a tiny, puzzled frown creasing her forehead. She was wondering how we spent the rest of the night, Lissa knew, and felt even more embarrassed.

Hugh leaned back comfortably in his chair. 'Lissa thrives on hard work, Maman. See how sprightly she looks this morning.'

'*I* think she looks a little tired,' his mother said, 'and I'm not going to allow you to work her again today. I shall put my foot down.'

'No need to get so fierce, Maman,' Hugh drawled. 'I didn't intend to work this morning anyway. I've promised to go in search of new lodgings for Carolyn, which will no doubt take me all morning and into the afternoon—unless I'm very lucky.'

'Good,' Monique said crisply, obviously pleased that Carolyn wouldn't be wished upon her for an indefinite stay. 'We're having an early meal this evening, before we leave for the private view. Claude will be at the gallery, of course. You'll be back in time to drive Lissa and me into town, Hugh?'

'Of course, Maman.' He got up and sketched a small bow. 'I shall look forward to the honour of escorting two beautiful ladies.'

His mother looked after him as he went out of the room, her bright eyes softening. 'My son,' she said to Lissa, 'is a very kind man. Spending all morning looking for digs for Carolyn indeed!'

Lissa buttered a croissant and said nothing. A kind man! Hugh? Well, yes, she supposed he could be kind. She remembered last night and how he had held her, soothed her, laughed away her fears.

Monique was pursuing her own train of thought. 'Surely the girl can do *something* for herself and not leave it all to him,' she muttered to herself in annoyance. She regarded Lissa wryly. 'Do I sound bitchy? I supposed I am where Carolyn is concerned. You see, I've been afraid for some time that she may succeed in capturing Hugh. Carolyn's a very pushy girl and what she's looking for is marriage. She's the daughter of Hugh's well-loved godfather, who died a few years ago. She was very young then and she had no other family. Hugh took on the responsibility for her.'

Lissa nodded. 'Yes, he told me.'

'Did he?' Monique brightened. 'Well, then, perhaps you'll know that my son is one of those men who take their responsibilities very seriously?'

'Yes.' She knew that too. Hadn't he taken the responsibility for her?

Monique went on, frowning down into her coffee-cup, 'I can't tell you how wonderful he was to me when things were going wrong between his father and me—taking over the company when he was so very young, working day and night to make sure it didn't collapse. Without his understanding and love I think I'd have gone under.'

There was a silence. Lissa sat very still, remembering Hugh's kindness and understanding to *her* last night. What a strange mixture he was—she doubted if she would ever really know him.

Monique looked up. 'That's why I worry about the way Carolyn's angling for him. You see, the girl went through a very bad time a year or two ago, and Hugh feels he should help her all he can. But she wouldn't be right for him. It would be a tragedy if he let himself be swayed by pity, and they say that pity is akin to love, don't they?' She smiled very ruefully. 'She leans on him and flatters him. Men are supposed to like that, aren't they?' She hesitated. 'So perhaps you can understand, Lissa, why I was so delighted when he phoned to say he was bringing you home with him. He's never brought a girl home before, and I thought——'

'Please,' Lissa broke in quickly. 'He only brought me because of my accident and I had nowhere to go, and he thought I could help him with his work. There's nothing—nothing else,' she finished lamely.

'Oh, dear, then I'm so sorry if I've jumped to the wrong conclusion and embarrassed you.'

If Monique was disappointed she was bearing up remarkably well. She said brightly, 'Now, what are we going to do with ourselves this morning? You should have some fun, as you've been working half the night. No visit to Paris is complete without seeing our famous shops, so shall we go into town and do some window-gazing?'

'Oh, yes, I'd love that.' To get right away from any chance of encountering Hugh, not to feel those strange silver-grey eyes fixed on her with a mocking light, as they had been more and more often recently—that would be a welcome reprieve.

'Good,' her hostess said briskly. 'Henri can drive us into the town. Henri is Marie's husband, you know, and he'll probably be quite glad to get away from the family reunion,' she added drily. 'We'll leave at ten o'clock, shall we? I simply adore shopping. We'll have such fun.'

It *was* fun. Lissa found Monique a delightful companion as they wandered round the glittering department stores and gazed in the windows of the exclusive shops of the Faubourg-St-Honoré.

'But the prices!' Lissa exclaimed, having done some mental arithmetic to convert francs into pounds. 'I'd never dare to go into one of these shops.'

'Wait!' Monique told her mysteriously. 'I have something to show you.' And Lissa was whisked through the crowds, down several small streets until at last they came to an unobtrusive glass door marked simply 'Louise'.

A tiny woman in a stylish black dress, with a single row of seed-pearls round her neck, came forward to meet them and greeted Monique in an enthusiastic flow of French of which Lissa couldn't understand a word. A long conversation followed while Lissa stood and waited, and at last the little woman led them through an archway into a small showroom beyond.

Lissa had expected to see a few outfits arranged with the same elegant sparseness as the window displays of the famous fashion shops in the boulevards. But here all was lavishness and profusion. Rails bulged with fabulous creations in every colour and texture and fabric. More exotic garments hung on hooks along the walls.

'Louise is quite famous,' Monique told Lissa in an undertone. 'Many of our Parisian socialites come here for their clothes.' She evidently intended to choose a new outfit for herself from this Aladdin's Cave of colour and beauty, Lissa thought. It would be fun to watch the proceedings.

The saleswoman was walking round Lissa, taking long, considering looks, murmuring comments in French to Monique, who turned to Lissa and said, 'Louise doesn't speak English, so perhaps I'd better do the talking, shall I? Tell her exactly the kind of dress it would be suitable for you to wear this evening.'

'For *me*?' Lissa gasped. 'But I thought—haven't you come to buy something for yourself?'

Monique smiled her secret little smile. 'Oh, no, I have all the clothes I need at present,' she said placidly. 'This is for you.'

'But Monique——' Lissa was horrified. These clothes would certainly be way beyond her budget. 'I really don't need a new dress, I have two cotton dresses that are quite pretty—and anyway, nobody is going to look at me.' But even as she said the words her eyes were passing in fascination and yearning over the bewildering assortment of gorgeous clothes displayed before her.

'A pretty girl always needs a new dress,' Monique told her in a tone that invited no argument. 'Put yourself in Louise's hands—she's a marvel.'

Louise had already started making a choice. She was muttering to herself as she swished hangers along the rail. 'What's she saying?' Lissa whispered.

Monique smiled, a wicked little smile, like someone plotting a satisfying *coup*. 'Something very complimentary, I promise you. For one thing, she's raving about the colour of your hair. It's rather unusual, you know. Not red, not gold, not brown, a subtle blend of them all. Very beautiful.'

Half an hour later Lissa's head was spinning and her arms ached with holding them over her head for one dress after another to be slipped on— summery affairs, but nothing like the little summer dresses she usually bought at home. These were exotic voiles and chiffons, sheers that revealed the body line beneath, cobwebby lace, colours like an artist's palette. Dresses for romantic evenings.

Louise gave a little grunt of satisfaction as she selected one that was her final choice. *'Voilà!'* She turned Lissa to the long cheval-glass for her approval.

Lissa hardly recognised herself in the tall, elegant girl she saw reflected there. The dress was of palest celery-green crêpe de Chine, with a ruched bodice that followed the soft curves of her breast and narrowed to her small waist. The wide shoulder-straps were embroidered in ivory, as was the bottom of the full, knee-skimming skirt. A wide scarf of ivory chiffon was thrown carelessly round her shoulders. The whole effect was simple and yet sophisticated, a dress she would never have dreamed of buying for herself in a hundred years. It was simply—Paris.

'Elle est ravissante—exquise!' Louise exulted. She gathered Lissa's curls up on to the top of her head and pushed a couple of hairpins in to hold them. Then she stood back, crooning with satisfaction.

Monique nodded confirmation. 'Yes, it's perfect. Quite delicious. *Mon Dieu,'* she sighed, smiling, 'how wonderful to be young. Do you like it?'

Lissa was speechless. She turned round slowly, trying to come to terms with the girl in the Paris dress who looked back at her from the mirror. 'I love it,' she croaked, when she had found her voice. 'But isn't it a bit—too much? I'm only Hugh's employee, you know, a lowly member of his company.'

Monique brushed that aside. 'This evening you're coming as one of the family, my dear. And Claude's openings are fairly dressed-up affairs. No, you must have it, you look very lovely, and we must give you an evening to remember as you've been working so hard in my son's interest.'

Lissa gave in. She might try to argue with Hugh, but she couldn't oppose his mother's wishes. A quick calculation assured her that her bank account would probably just about stand the strain, and a few minutes later she left the boutique beside Monique, carrying a pink dress-box with the magic word 'Paris' printed on it in small letters, under the scrawled 'Louise'. The dress had been entered to Monique's account. She would settle up later.

'We shall go to the Galeries Lafayette for your sandals,' Monique announced, 'and after that find a café for a light lunch. I don't care for a heavy meal in the middle of the day, do you? How does that sound?'

'It sounds marvellous,' agreed Lissa. She was under the spell of Paris by now and would have agreed to anything.

Half an hour later she had collected two more carrier-bags—one containing a pair of strappy sandals in ivory kid with little gold buckles, and the other a lacy white shawl—'in case the evening turns cold,' Monique had advised.

Then it was time for a light lunch—an omelette with a glass of chilled white wine—at an open-air café shaded by a vast red and white striped canopy. After they had finished the meal, Monique confessed to feeling a little tired and asked the waiter to find a taxi to take them home.

When they arrived there Lissa carried her parcels into the wide, cool hall and turned to Monique. 'Thank you so much, *madame*. It's been a lovely morning.'

'It's been a pleasure, my dear. I've missed out on having a daughter to buy pretty things for.'

'I'm thrilled with my dress. May I settle up now?' As Lissa put down her parcels and opened her handbag to get her cheque book out, Monique put a hand on hers.

'Please let me, my dear. It will give me such delight to see you looking beautiful this evening. And I did bully you into buying the dress. Now we won't argue about it, shall we? I'm going to have my after-lunch siesta.'

Suddenly she gave a little gasp and pressed her hands to her stomach. She had gone very pale.

'What is it, *madame*? Aren't you well?'

Monique drew in a long breath and screwed up her eyes for a moment. Then she opened them with a sigh of relief. 'Gone now. I probably ate my omelette too fast. I'm perfectly all right now.'

'Are you *sure*?' Lissa said anxiously.

Monique touched her cheek lightly. 'Quite sure. I sometimes get these little turns, it's nothing. I shall go and have a good rest and I suggest you do the same. Shopping is tiring. We'll meet for a light meal before we get ready to leave, shall we? At six o'clock? Run along now, and don't worry about me—I'm fine.'

By half-past six Lissa had slept for a couple of hours, joined her hostess—who, to Lissa's relief, seemed quite herself again—for a light meal, and learned that Hugh had returned to say that he had found new digs for Carolyn, and had come home to collect her cases. He was expected back in time to drive them into Paris.

Lissa laid the green dress out on the bed and touched its silken folds delicately, wondering for the hundredth time why Monique had insisted on playing fairy godmother to a girl she scarcely knew. There was only one answer that made sense. She intended Lissa to dazzle Hugh and put Carolyn in the shade. Lissa smiled wryly. Madame didn't know half the story, did she? She wasn't sure she knew the whole story herself. But one thing stood out with painful clarity: nothing had changed. She was almost painfully in love with Hugh, and Hugh was in love with his computer, and only needed a girl to satisfy his physical desires.

From the beginning he had put her in a false position here, and nothing that had happened today had changed that. She'd been a fool, she told herself with self-disgust. She'd been weak enough to let herself be manipulated by Hugh, and now, more gently, by his mother. To be *used*.

It was humiliating. There was no future for her in staying here. No future in dressing up to impress Hugh this evening. She wouldn't go, she thought defiantly. She'd plead a bad headache and stay behind.

Then her glance fell upon the green dress. Monique had really enjoyed helping to choose it for her, whatever the reason, and it would be churlish and ungrateful to disappoint her. Monique had said she would be going as one of the family. Very well, she would *be* one of the family. The humble guinea-pig would be transformed into a glamorous princess—and if the prince didn't even notice the change at least it would be exciting to wear a beautiful dress like this for its own sake. Stripping off the suit and blouse she had worn all day, she walked briskly into the shower-room.

There was plenty of time to wash her hair and have a leisurely shower. Lissa loved the masculine appointments of the room—all in indigo blue. She wondered if Hugh had chosen the colour scheme himself—it was cool, just as he was. Cool and a little mysterious, like being at the bottom of the sea.

Which wasn't a bad analogy, she reflected, as she towel-dried her hair after her shower. Certainly she was way out of her depth here.

The housekeeper had evidently removed Hugh's toilet things when the rooms had been changed and substituted a feminine variety. Monique must have chosen them all—creams and lotions, shampoos, moisturising gels, toilet water. Lissa revelled in the cosseted luxury and the ravishing smell as she smoothed body lotion on to her soft skin. This was a far cry from her small bedroom at home with its modest equipment of pots and bottles. Soon she would be back there, perhaps dressing for a tennis club dance or an evening at the ice-rink. She tried to believe it would be the same as it had always been, but she knew it wouldn't. Nothing would be the same again. No man would stir her pulses and make the blood race in her veins as Hugh did, merely by looking at her, speaking to her.

When she couldn't make the enjoyable ritual of the shower last any longer she wrapped a fleecy dark blue bath towel round her and opened the door into the bedroom.

Then the breath left her body. Hugh was standing in front of the open wardrobe cupboard, wearing a burgundy silk robe, pushing aside her selection of clothes. He looked round as Lissa emerged from the shower-room and his grey eyes narrowed as they lingered on the long, long legs showing beneath the towel. 'Well, well, a pleasure to meet you here, Miss Stephens.'

She drew the towel closer. 'Well, it's not a pleasure to meet you, Mr Winchester. What are you doing in my room?'

'Actually it does happen to be *my* room, and I'm looking for an evening suit, which Maman insists upon my wearing for this evening's shindig. I did knock,' he added mildly.

'All right, then—well, please take it and go,' she said ungraciously. It would be naïve to scuttle back to the shower-room, which was what she would have liked to do.

She felt the heat rising into her cheeks as he continued to inspect her quite shamelessly. 'And unless I'm mistaken,' he murmured, taking a couple of steps towards her, 'that happens to be one of my towels you're wearing so delightfully.' He picked up a corner of the blue towel and inspected the label. 'Ah, yes, certainly one of mine.'

Lissa grabbed the towel away from him and in so doing let go of the top she was holding round herself. The result was inevitable. The towel slipped downwards, disclosing a pair of deliciously creamy breasts.

'Oh,' she gasped furiously, trying to rearrange it. 'This is really ridiculous.'

The grey eyes creased into a smile. 'Oh, I wouldn't say ridiculous,' he said. 'I'd have other words—like enchanting, bewitching, enthralling.'

Suddenly he wasn't smiling any more. He was standing close in front of her, and she tried to take a step backwards but her legs refused to move. She was feverishly conscious that underneath the silk gown he was naked. She was also conscious that he was undoubtedly aroused.

'Go away,' she gasped.

The grey eyes had darkened. 'I can't,' he said simply. 'I'm afraid I must have something, if it's only a kiss.'

As his arms came round her the towel dropped away, but she hardly noticed. She was totally unable to resist him, consumed by such wanton desire as she had never imagined. His mouth ravaged hers and she gave him back kiss for kiss, straining against the hardness of his body beneath the silk robe. His mouth left hers and travelled burningly down to fasten on the swollen peak of her breast, and a thrill that was almost painful quivered through her.

'Lissa—please,' he pleaded hoarsely against her lips, easing her backwards to the bed. 'We could be so good together. I'd make you forget that bastard Paul, I promise.'

Afterwards, she never knew whether it was the way he spoke the name, or the way the silky crêpe of the dress on the bed touched her bare legs, reminding her of the time and place. But, whichever it was, she was suddenly back in the real world and she had to dress and make up and be ready to leave when Monique called her.

She summoned all her strength and pushed him away. 'This is quite mad.' She picked up the towel and draped it round herself again. 'Have you forgotten we're due to go out to a social occasion with your mother in a few minutes?' She could hear Hugh's breathing, quick and desperate, but she couldn't bear to look at his face. 'You've had your kiss—now run along and leave me to get ready.'

He walked away to stare out of the window, where the light was quickly fading. At last he turned with a wry attempt at a smile. 'Sensible Lissa!' he said. 'Perhaps after all you're the reasonable one. Thanks for reminding me.'

He went across to the wardrobe and took down the dark blue evening suit from the end of the rail. Then he smiled at her and she could see the effort he was making to behave naturally.

'That your dress for this evening?' He glanced at the green crêpe confection on the bed.

It was Lissa's turn to appear normal. 'Lovely, isn't it? Your mother persuaded me to buy it this morning. She wants to make me a present of it, but I can't possibly accept it of course.' Her laugh sounded abysmally affected in her ears. 'Perhaps you'd explain to her? I'd hate to seem ungrateful, I like your mother so very much.'

He eased the evening suit over his arm on its hanger as he walked to the door. 'She likes you. She's got you lined up as a future daughter-in-law.'

'Oh, *no*!' Her voice rose several semitones. 'Then you'll have to do even more explaining to her. Doesn't she know that you've decided against marriage? Logically, of *course*.'

He walked to the door. From that distance they eyed each other. Lissa waited for some biting put-down. He wasn't a man to be needled. But he merely hitched the suit further over his arm and opened the door. 'See you later,' he said, and went out.

CHAPTER EIGHT

'WE'RE a little late.' Monique, elegant in a classic black silk suit, waited with Lissa as Hugh parked his car conveniently close to the gallery. 'That's as it should be.' There was a wicked gleam in her dark eyes as she whispered to Lissa, 'You will make an entrance, my dear. You look lovely.'

'Thanks to you.' Lissa smiled, catching sight of herself in the large plate-glass window of the gallery. The tall girl in the cool green dress seemed like a stranger. It was a very odd feeling. Monique had sent Marie to help Lissa arrange her hair. Marie, it seemed, had been a hairdresser before her marriage and she wielded a styling brush with expertise. Lissa's tawny curls were taken straight back and piled on top of her head in a complicated fashion. Marie had been in raptures over the result, standing back to admire her handiwork in a flood of French, of which Lissa could only get the general drift. All she could do was beam and say carefully, *'Merci, madame, vous êtes très gentille,'* which had seemed to please the housekeeper.

Having locked the car, Hugh joined his mother and Lissa. He walked between them into the gallery, and the touch of his hand at her elbow sent a shock wave up Lissa's arm and made her stumble against him.

She pulled away with a quick apology and saw his wicked sideways glance. With his dark hair

sleeked back he looked very French tonight and very
gorgeous in the indigo-blue suit and white silk shirt,
as she had known he would. She felt a tremor run
through her and braced herself against it. She'd
have to get over this crazy, desperate longing for
the man. She had to keep on reminding herself that
if she accepted his 'proposition' it would be sexual
satisfaction for him and nothing more. For her it
would be a brief, dizzy flight up to the stars and
then a long, sickening slump into endless black
misery.

'You're shivering.' He leaned his dark head down
to hers. 'Not feeling nervous?'

'A little, perhaps. This is a new kind of occasion
for me and I don't know anything about modern
art.' That was as good an excuse as any.

He squeezed her arm. 'You don't have to. I certainly don't. Nobody looks at the pictures at a
private view. And when they see you they won't
want to look at pictures anyway. Did I tell you you
look quite ravishing?'

She laughed brightly. 'The humble guinea-pig
transformed into a princess?'

'*My* guinea-pig, therefore *my* princess. That
follows. I shall protect my princess from any lech-
erous advances from other males.'

He was joking, of course, but there was something—something proprietorial in his voice that
made her heart leap, and his arm had slipped down
to her waist as they entered the main gallery.

The gallery was transformed from the way it had
been yesterday. Large, strikingly coloured pictures
were hung at wide intervals on the white walls. Elegant women and their menfolk stood about in

groups, wine glasses in hand. A few people were walking round, seriously examining the pictures, but most were talking and laughing and the air was full of the buzz of conversation and wafts of French perfume.

At the far end of the room stood a long table stacked with bottles of wine and bowls of olives and snacks. Philippe, Claude's young assistant, was dispensing drinks, assisted by Carolyn, wearing a pale yellow sleeveless all-in-one, which shimmered in the spot-lighting and showed every delicate curve of her body. Her silver-gilt hair hung straight down round her exquisite, small face. She looked young and vulnerable and Lissa could well understand Monique's anxiety that Carolyn would at some stage get under Hugh's defences and that his affection might turn to something deeper.

Perhaps she was right, Lissa thought gloomily.

Carolyn's eyes were travelling restlessly round the room as she poured wine, and when she saw Hugh, with Lissa beside him, her arm jerked and the red wine slopped over the glass and spilled on to the white cloth. She made a movement as if she would run to Hugh, but Philippe handed her a cloth and she began sulkily to mop up the spill.

'Oh, dear, trouble,' murmured Hugh. 'I'll go and get us drinks,' and he hurried across the room. He took the cloth from Carolyn and began to rub at the stain himself, laughing into her limpid blue eyes, and saying something that drew a grateful, wistful smile from her.

Claude emerged from a group and came forward to greet his wife, kissing her on both cheeks and then kissing Lissa similarly. 'My two very beautiful ladies,' he said huskily, his wicked dark eyes dancing with pleasure. One of the family, indeed! Lissa thought, half amused, half regretful that it wasn't true.

'Now you must come and meet people.' Claude put a drink into her hand. He radiated energy and enthusiasm. The evening was obviously going well.

Monique was busy greeting old acquaintances, passing from group to group, and Lissa found herself being presented by Claude as 'a very dear friend of my stepson, Hugh—from England'. She could feel interested eyes looking her over—the women's calculating, the men's with a smiling, blatant message that made the heat come into her cheeks. Most of them spoke in French and she couldn't understand much of what was being said, but it didn't really matter because as more and more visitors crowded into the gallery the decibels rose higher and higher, until everyone seemed to be shrieking at once with the greatest good humour.

Lissa looked round for Hugh. He was still standing at the drinks table, talking to Carolyn. She hesitated, half wishing she were like Carolyn, who would run across and take his arm and smile up at him possessively. Presumably that was what he would wish *her* to do, if she were to act in character in his silly charade. No, she thought, watching his head bend over the girl's silver-gilt hair, I'm darned if I will. Let him solve his own problems.

Claude was beside her. 'You must meet our artist, Lissa.' He added confidentially, 'The young man is a little *anxieux*. This is his first show, you understand.'

That makes two of us, Lissa thought, as Claude led her across the room towards a lanky young man with cropped black hair, wearing a very new-looking plum-coloured velvet suit.

Claude introduced him as Jacques Garard. 'Lissa does not speak French, Jacques, so you may practise your English.' He left them together.

The young artist's dreamy dark eyes lit up as they rested on Lissa. 'You like my pictures a little, yes?' he asked diffidently.

She smiled at him. 'I haven't been able to get a good look at them yet,' she said. 'Will you take me round and tell me about them?'

Jacques agreed immediately and led Lissa from picture to picture, standing back to watch her reaction.

'There are more in the small gallery. Let us go in there,' he urged, putting a hand rather timidly on her arm.

The small gallery was empty except for one elderly gentleman who was having a gentle snooze on a chair in the middle of the room. Three large canvases adorned the wall.

Lissa paused in front of the first one. '*Eh bien?* What do you think?' Jacques gazed at her eagerly.

'Oh, yes, I like them a lot.' Lissa looked rather blankly at the enormous painting of red blobs against a swirling blue-green background, wondering what to say. 'But I'm afraid I don't really understand...'

Then at last the penny dropped. She gave a little squeal of delight. 'Ah, I *see* now. They are apples. Green apples, red apples, yellow apples. They are what you call "still life", aren't they?'

Jacques was enchanted. 'You are very clever, *mademoiselle*. I wish all my friends are as clever.' He beamed happily on her. 'Yes, they are "still life", or as we call it, *"nature morte"*.'

'Dead nature? But they look so alive, so vivid.'

'That is what my pictures are about, *mademoiselle*. But I could not explain them so quickly and easily.' He hesitated. 'I should be honoured if *mademoiselle* would find time to visit me in my studio and then I could perhaps show her more pictures—tell her of my ideas?' The young man searched Lissa's face hopefully.

Behind them Hugh's voice broke in, addressing the artist in his own language, and both Jacques and Lissa spun round. Lissa didn't understand what Hugh said, but she recognised the chill in his voice and she saw the colour run up into Jacques's pale cheeks.

He made her a little, apologetic bow. 'Forgive me, *mademoiselle*, I did not understand.' He smiled rather pathetically. 'Thank you for looking at my pictures,' he said, and went back into the main gallery.

Hugh glowered down at Lissa. 'So this is what you get up to when my back is turned?'

The remark was so ridiculous that she waited for him to smile, but his mouth was a straight, disapproving line.

'Don't be ridiculous.' Lissa glared back at him. 'I was taking an interest in the pictures—which is more than you seem to be doing.'

'Oh, yes? I gather that you'd got to the stage of "come up and look at my etchings". Quick work!'

He really was annoyed. Lissa's heart missed a beat—was it possible that he was jealous?

'I shan't answer that,' she said, lifting her chin loftily. 'You're being too petty for words. Please take my glass.' She handed him her empty wine glass and swept towards the large gallery.

Before she could get there his hand closed on her arm. 'Do you really want to look at any more pictures? I've had enough. I've told Maman we're going to sneak out for a while—come along.'

Lissa's heart beat a little tattoo. It would be heaven to stroll by the river in the cool of the evening with Hugh at her side. She allowed herself to be led through the lobby and out into the street.

Outside, Hugh made for the car and unlocked the doors. 'You've seen Paris by day, now see it lit up.' He smiled. He was recovering his good humour now that they were out of the gallery. 'Let's have a run round.'

That, thought Lissa, would be even more exciting. And it was. As the car swished along the smooth avenues among all the other cars, she sat back and loved every minute of it, tucking it away in her memory to gloat over afterwards.

Paris was magical at night. Everything was bathed in light—the trees, lawns, the flower-beds, the fabulous buildings. Lissa was entranced. She could have purred like a kitten surrounded by saucers of cream as each new aspect of beauty revealed itself.

Hugh had to attend to his driving, but he listed the names of some of the famous places as they drove along the Champs Elysées, to the Arc de Triomphe, round a huge traffic island adorned with fountains that flashed like diamonds in the lights, to the Place de la Concorde where lamps and spotlights glowed like giant fireflies and more fountains sent their glittering jets high into the night sky.

'It's like fairyland,' murmured Lissa.

Hugh said wryly, 'Now it is, perhaps, but it hasn't always been like this. This is the spot where the guillotine did its dastardly work. But your tender heart won't want to dwell on that, Lissa. Have a look at the obelisk glorifying Rameses II which they put in its place.' He lifted a hand briefly to indicate a tall, slender pillar, golden in the floodlights. As they passed, Lissa could make out the Egyptian engravings which disappeared into the shadows at the top of the column.

She sighed with pleasure. 'In spite of its gory bits of history, I think Paris is the most beautiful city in the world.'

Hugh chuckled. 'Being half-French, I half agree with you. And there's lots more you haven't seen— we must come back often.'

Lissa slid a quick glance at his profile, etched against the lights outside; the strong, dominant nose, the square chin, the mouth firmed as he wove in and out of the ceaseless traffic. He had said that so easily as if there were a future that held both of them. She had to remind herself that there was no chance of that, so she might as well make the most of this fantastic evening.

'Paris is at its best at night,' Hugh was saying. 'It's not called the City of Light for nothing—which gives me another idea. Hold on to your seat, Lissa, we're going to make for the Pont de l'Alma, which is where the river-boats start from.'

If the drive round the city had been magic, the river trip was pure heaven. Hugh wrapped Lissa's shawl round her shoulders and left his arm there, pulling her comfortably against him as they sat on a seat on the deck, watching the river-bank slip by, illuminated by the boat's own searchlights.

At first Hugh identified some of the more spectacular buildings. 'We go a little way upstream first to see the Eiffel Tower. Look, there it is——' he drew her closer as they neared the famous landmark, which thrust its floodlit iron lattices into the black velvet of the sky '—rather splendid, don't you think? Now we turn and go downstream, past the Gare d'Orsay and the Institut de France—and look, here's Notre Dame again, in her beautiful mantle of floodlights...'

Lissa let herself relax against him, her head on his shoulder, and his voice came dreamily into her consciousness. Nothing was really registering now except the bliss of this moment. She was filled with a deep sense of contentment, of the rightness of being here with him, the two of them together with everyone else shut out, their bodies pressed together so closely.

Sounds came from a long distance away—the hum of traffic from the *quai*, the chatter of the other passengers, the lapping of the water below. It seemed inevitable when Hugh's mouth came down to hers in a long, unforgettable kiss. She kissed him back, loving him so much that it felt almost like pain. She couldn't go on like this, she thought, she must take whatever he had to offer and risk the consequences. Tonight—when they got home...

He might have guessed her thoughts. His question was almost inaudible as he breathed close to her ear, 'Is it yes, Lissa? Later?'

For answer she drew even closer and lifted her mouth again for his kiss. She was committed now, there was no way she could change her mind.

Back in the car Lissa took her mirror and comb from her handbag and tried to persuade her hair into place.

Hugh said reluctantly, 'I suppose we'd better show up at the gallery again. They won't have left yet.'

Lissa gasped. 'I can't, I must look a mess. My hair...'

'Your hair is very beautiful. I can't wait to take the pins out and see it fall into my hands,' he whispered. She couldn't wait either—the hot blood was running recklessly through her body.

After he started the engine Hugh leaned over and kissed her again, very gently and slowly, and his kiss was a promise. He took a loose tendril of her hair between his fingers and kissed that too. 'Who said I wasn't a romantic?' He laughed, and began to back the car out of its parking space.

They were at the gallery again much too soon. Lissa hadn't had time to come back to earth when Hugh was helping her out of the car and leading her inside, an arm around her waist. 'We won't have to put on an act for Carolyn's benefit,' he said. 'This is for real.'

For real! But for how long? Lissa dared not think about that.

The number of visitors had thinned out, but there were still a few remaining. The first thing Lissa noticed when they re-entered the gallery was that several of the pictures had little red stickers beside them. Oh, good! That nice boy had sold some of his pictures—he would be over the moon.

Then she forgot all about pictures as she felt Hugh's hand suddenly grip her arm so tightly that it hurt and heard his outraged snarl of profanity. He was staring across the room, his face darkly furious. Lissa followed his gaze. Leaning nonchalantly against the drinks table, his eyes following Carolyn as she cleared away glasses with shaking hands, was Paul.

Paul spotted Hugh and Lissa and loped across to them immediately. He turned his charismatic smile on Lissa, put his arms round her and kissed her enthusiastically. 'Hello, sweetheart, how goes it? I heard you were lending a hand over here.'

Hugh pushed roughly in front of Lissa, as if he wanted to protect her. His face was white and ominously grim. 'What the hell are you doing here?'

'Looking for you, old boy,' Paul said amiably. 'I've got some news that I think will interest you.' He glanced back towards Carolyn. 'And renewing old acquaintances at the same time.' He grinned. 'One meets one's friends in all sorts of unexpected places.'

Hugh's hands clenched. Oh, lord, thought Lissa, There's going to be a fight. The worst thing was that she didn't know why.

'Don't worry, I'm not planning to park myself on you,' Paul went on. 'I've got a room at a nice little pub just round the corner—the Danube. How about if you come along there with me now? We can't talk here.'

Hugh was keeping his temper under control with a tremendous effort. 'I've not the slightest wish to talk to you,' he snapped. 'You've got a bloody nerve to turn up here.'

Paul managed to look wryly apologetic. 'Sorry, chum, but time is of the essence. I tried to contact you at your home and your housekeeper told me you were here, so here I am. It really is urgent, I promise you—won't wait until tomorrow.'

Hugh drew in an exasperated breath. 'I suppose I'd better come with you, then.' He turned to Lissa with a shrug. 'You see how it is. I'll be back as soon as I can.'

Paul was all smiles now that he had got his own way. 'Be seeing you, Lissa,' he grinned, touching her cheek. 'There's lots to tell you.'

'You can cut that out.' Hugh was fast nearing boiling-point. 'Come on, blast you, if you're coming.' He stalked to the door.

Paul pulled a face towards Lissa and followed Hugh out of the gallery.

Well, what now? Lissa thought disconsolately, looking around for Monique or Claude, neither of whom was to be seen. Philippe was clearing up at the drinks table, helped by an obviously reluctant Carolyn.

Then Claude came out of the office and made straight for Lissa. He took her arm and pulled her aside. 'Monique is feeling very unwell,' he said in a low, worried voice. 'I am going to drive her home immediately. I have telephoned to her doctor and he will meet us there. She would like you to come with us and look after her on the way, Lissa, if you will, please.'

'Of course.' Lissa fought down her alarm. 'I'll come at once.'

Claude hurried towards the office, asking over his shoulder, 'Do you know where Hugh is?'

'His stepbrother turned up unexpectedly and Hugh has gone with him to his hotel. Some business they had to discuss.'

Monique was alone in the office, doubled up over the table. Her face was haggard; she looked old and ill. She raised her head with an attempt at a smile as Lissa went in. 'It's this wretched pain again—stupid, isn't it?'

Lissa went down on one knee and took her hand and held it tightly. It was icy cold. 'We'll soon have you home, and your doctor will be there,' she said in what she hoped was an encouraging tone. Actually she was appalled by Monique's appearance. And why wasn't Hugh here? He'd be shattered when he found out.

Claude drove carefully on the way home and Lissa sat close to Monique on the wide back seat, holding her hands, not talking much but trying to give comfort just by being there.

The drive seemed to take longer than usual, but at last they were there and the doctor's car was pulled up before the house.

Lissa's part was over now. Claude and the doctor helped Monique into the salon and closed the door. Lissa sat down on a bench in the hall and waited.

Marie appeared from the back quarters, flapping her hands enquiringly. Lissa searched in her memory for the words. She pointed towards the closed door and said, *'Madame est malade.'*

'Mon Dieu!' The housekeeper cast her eyes to heaven but she didn't seem altogether surprised. Perhaps, Lissa thought, she had been expecting it.

A few minutes later Claude came out and spoke urgently to Marie, who hurried away upstairs. Then he came across the hall to Lissa. Tension was etching deep lines on his face but he spoke steadily. 'The doctor has phoned for an ambulance. It will be here very soon. I must find Hugh to tell him— can you tell me where he went?'

Lissa screwed up her eyes, trying to remember what Paul had said. 'The hotel was—was—yes, I remember now. It was the Danube.'

'The Danube. *Oui*, I know it. Thank you, *ma chère*.' He stopped for a moment, regarding her pale, perturbed face. Then he patted her hand. 'We must hope for the best, must we not?'

Lissa looked after him with tears scalding her eyes as he walked rapidly back to his wife. Then she went slowly to her room. She heard the ambulance arrive and leave again. Then she sat down on the bed to wait. There was nothing else to do.

The worst thing, in all the hours that followed, was not knowing anything. Not the name of the hospital, not what was happening there, not if Monique was holding her own. If she could have talked to Marie it might have helped. When she got back to London, she vowed, she'd take up learning French seriously. Although—what was the point? She wouldn't be coming back here as 'one of the family', would she?

By midnight it seemed clear that neither Claude nor Hugh would return tonight. Lissa undressed and got into bed, leaving the communicating door with the office wide open in case the telephone rang.

It seemed a lifetime ago since she had sat on the deck of the river-boat with Hugh's arms round her and he had murmured, 'Later?' Perhaps she had been saved from doing something very stupid and she should be glad. But instead she longed for him—here—beside her in this big bed, with a longing that was slowly sending her crazy.

Somehow the night passed. She slept for short, uneasy periods and wakened again, her heart thumping. As soon as it got light she got up and showered and dressed and went into the office.

Marie brought her breakfast and said something in French, gesturing excitedly, and although Lissa couldn't understand the words the sense came through clear and strong.

'No.' Lissa shook her head, indicating the telephone. 'I haven't heard anything yet.' The housekeeper shrugged almost angrily and went away.

All morning Lissa worked in the office, trying not to think of what was happening in some unknown hospital. She kept on telling herself that no news was good news but, like other pat sayings intended to uplift, it didn't work when put to the test.

She stared blindly at the words on the screen. Hugh was so devoted to his mother—what would happen to the launch of his new machine if—if...? She wouldn't think of that, she *wouldn't*.

It was after ten o'clock that night when Hugh walked in. Lissa jumped up, searching his face to read some message there, good or bad. He slumped into his chair by the desk. He looked terrible—his face was grey with fatigue and there were purple shadows under his eyes.

Lissa went across and touched his shoulder. 'Please tell me what's happened, I don't know anything.'

He raised bloodshot eyes. 'It was an emergency operation but they got it in time. They think she'll be——' his voice broke '—all right.'

Lissa pressed her cheek against his hair and his arm came round her waist, drawing her against him. 'It's been a bloody awful time,' he muttered.

Marie had evidently heard Hugh's car arrive and now she came hurrying into the office, firing agitated questions at him. When he gave her what must have been reassurance, she burst into another torrent of words. Finally, waving her hands, she disappeared towards the kitchen.

'She's a good soul and she's very fond of my mother. She's going to get me some sandwiches,' Hugh said wearily. 'Now be a sweet girl, and fetch me a drink.'

She went to the cupboard and mixed a large whisky and water. By now she knew just how he liked it.

'Thanks.' He drank it off. 'That's better.' He put down his glass on the desk. 'Lord, I'm tired.'

She said, 'You need to sleep. Lie down on your own bed, you'll be more comfortable there.'

'You don't mind?'

'Don't be silly, of course I don't. Come on.' She took his hand and he stumbled into the bedroom after her and sank on to the bed.

Lissa took off his shoes and pulled the duvet up a little way. 'There, now sleep.'

He reached for her again and drew her down beside him. 'Don't go away,' he murmured. 'I like to feel you near me.'

Lissa heard Marie come into the office—presumably with the sandwiches—and go out again. Then she got up and closed the bedroom door and, pulling off her sandals and outer clothes, she snuggled down beside Hugh, who was already fast asleep, breathing regularly.

She lay very still for a long time, and when Hugh gave a little grunt and turned over towards her every muscle went tense. But he was still deeply asleep. One arm came out and rested heavily across her ribs and Lissa sighed and relaxed, letting herself slip further into the hollow made by his body. Last night, if things had gone right, they would have been in this bed together, but they would have been making love. For a while, nestling against him, she let herself imagine what it would have been like. She reached up and touched his hair, and the skin of his forehead was smooth and slightly damp. A long shiver ran through her. Oh, lord, she wasn't going to be able to bear it, wanting him so much.

Sleep was miles away. She was weak with a soft, sensuous longing that churned inside her. If she turned towards him—put her arms round him— would he wake up and want her?

Then suddenly realisation hit her like a blow. She was indulging herself in erotic fantasies while Hugh's mother was desperately ill, perhaps lying between life and death.

She was consumed by guilt. How could she have been so disgustingly insensitive? Holding her breath, she eased away from under Hugh's arm and slid out of the bed, shivering in the sudden chill. She waited a moment, but Hugh was still breathing deeply and evenly, so she picked up her clothes and tiptoed across the bedroom into the office next door, where she pulled out the camp-bed and prepared to spend a sleepless night—alone.

CHAPTER NINE

TOWARDS dawn Lissa dropped into a deep, unrefreshing sleep, and when she woke it was full daylight. She lay for a moment as the memory of what had happened filtered into her muzzy brain. Then she heard sounds from the shower-room next door and she shot out of bed, pulled on jeans and top, and raked fingers through her tumble of curls.

Presently Hugh came into the office. He was wearing nothing but a large blue bath towel round his waist, and his face was set in that grim expression that Lissa hated but recognised very well.

'I'm afraid I'll have to ask you to remove yourself while I dress,' he said stiffly. 'My clothes are in there.' He nodded towards a tall cupboard in the corner of the office.

Lissa didn't reply; she went into the bedroom and closed the door. What had happened to the man who had clung to her last night, who had seemed to need her? Biting her lip, she set about tidying the room and straightening the bed. In the shower-room the shirt Hugh had been wearing yesterday had fallen behind the bathroom stool. She picked it up and for a moment buried her face in its still-warm folds, which smelled so potently of the man himself. Then she pushed it into the linen basket, where Hugh had already deposited the rest of his clothes for Marie to deal with.

She was brushing her hair when he came into the room, dressed in a lightweight grey suit and white shirt, hair brushed immaculately. Only the dark blue tie, knotted clumsily with its end sticking out over the lapel of his jacket, gave evidence that he was under any sort of strain.

He said, not looking at Lissa, 'Sorry you were deprived of your bed last night. I take it you didn't think fit to share it with me,' he added distantly.

'I—I . . .' gulped Lissa, but he wasn't listening.

'I'm leaving now,' he said. 'Going first to the hospital to check on things there and hope they'll let me see Maman. Claude won't be coming back here for a couple of days at least. He'll be spending the nights at the gallery, to be near the hospital. As for myself, if I have a satisfactory report from the doctors, I plan to fly to London. I have to contact various people about——' for the first time his composure slipped for a moment '—about an urgent matter connected with my stepbrother. I shall have to leave you to get on with the final part of the work on your own.'

Lissa had got to her feet in front of the dressing-table, and stood facing him. 'Yes,' she said, and almost added 'sir', but she couldn't risk sarcasm.

'Right,' he said curtly. 'I'll be off, then. Probably be back on Wednesday.'

'Yes,' she said again, and as he turned to the door, 'Hugh . . .?'

He spun round, and in the sunlight that poured in through the window the grey eyes glittered into hers.

'Just——' Lissa faltered. 'I'm so sorry about your mother, I hope she'll be all right.'

He nodded. 'Thank you.'

'I'll want to know how she is. Is there some number I can ring?'

'You can ring Claude at the gallery,' he said shortly. 'The number's in the book.'

He went out of the room and a minute or so later Lissa heard the sound of his car engine starting up and fading away down the drive. She sank on to the dressing-stool, leaning forward as if she had received a punch in the stomach. That would have been almost preferable to the treatment she had just received from Hugh.

It couldn't have been made plainer to her that she might have been of use to him in his bed when he'd wakened, and that he was peeved that she hadn't stayed there. Apart from that he wanted nothing from her—not sympathy, not understanding. So there was nothing left for her here. Nothing. Nothing.

Except, she thought bitterly, to finish her work on the manual, and that she would do to the best of her ability. Then she would arrange to leave. She would arrange it very carefully, very methodically. Hugh would be proud of her, she thought bitterly.

She counted the francs in her purse. Monique had helped her to change some money on the day they'd gone shopping. That should be enough to pay for a taxi, when she finally left.

In a small room—obviously Claude's study—she found what she was looking for. Claude must have been working on his English when he'd married Hugh's mother, and among the books on his bookshelves were several textbooks, a dictionary, and a phrase book for visitors to France.

Taking the phrase book, Lissa went back to the office. The plate of sandwiches Marie had brought in last night were still on the desk, their edges curling up dejectedly. She would take them out into the garden later, and feed them to the birds.

She sat down at her own work-table and began to study the phrase book. A few minutes later she had found what she wanted and written it all down in her notebook with the translations into French. I shall be leaving at... Will you please call me a taxi...? Thank you very much for your kindness...

The last phrase—I have enjoyed myself very much—could safely be left out. There had been magic moments, but that was all they had been—moments. Nothing real, nothing lasting.

But if Monique hadn't been taken ill, there would have been more magic moments—in Hugh's arms. She was suddenly engulfed by a black tide of misery and inside was a great lump in her throat that wouldn't go away. Even if it hadn't lasted long she would have had that bliss to remember. What a cowardly fool she'd been to refuse him. She loved him so frantically that it was a pain inside her; she should have been brave enough to take what he'd offered. And now she had nothing. She laid her arms on the table and buried her head in them and wept.

A knock on the door made her start up, digging her fists in her eyes like a small child. Marie walked in with breakfast for two on a tray. She put it down on Hugh's desk and frowned at the dried-up plate of sandwiches. Then she stared at Lissa's wet cheeks and swollen eyes.

Lissa searched her mind for her O-level French and found very little. *'Monsieur Hugh est—est parti—en Angleterre,'* she tried, holding out her arms to indicate an aeroplane.

'Ah, oui.' Marie nodded sagely. She poured out a cup of very black coffee and handed it to Lissa and her dark, beady little eyes were kind. She probably knew all about young girls in love, Lissa thought. The French, she had heard, were more practical about these matters.

More sensible, she told herself, when Marie had gone. And she must be sensible too and not wallow in self-pity. She must have the work on the manual finished by the time Hugh returned—earlier if possible, then she could get away and wouldn't have to see him again. Grimly, Lissa mopped her eyes, drank her coffee, switched on the computer and began work.

She worked for the whole day, with short breaks for meals and a few minutes spent in the garden. It was another glorious spring day and Henri, Marie's husband, was busy weeding and keeping the garden in its usual immaculate condition. He stood up as she approached, leaning on his fork, his rubbery nut-brown face enigmatic. He seemed to be weighing her up and she wondered what Marie had told him about her.

She waved an arm, indicating the trim flower-beds. *'Très belle.'* She nodded and smiled encouragingly, and Henri pursed his lips, pushed back his black beret and suddenly grinned delightfully at her.

It wasn't so difficult after all, she thought, returning to the office. She ought to be able to make him understand about getting her a taxi when the time came.

In the middle of the day she searched the phone book for Claude's number at the gallery, and after a struggle with the unfamiliar routine managed to get through to him.

'Hugh said I could call you for news of *madame*,' she said tentatively.

Claude sounded tired but optimistic. He had just come from the hospital, he said, and the doctors were satisfied. 'I was able to stay with Monique for a few minutes—she is very cheerful. She asked me to thank you for looking after her, and I myself must also thank you, *ma petite*.'

He went on a little longer. Monique would like to see her when she was able to receive more visitors. Hugh had flown to London, he understood, but would be back when his business was completed. She was comfortable at the house, he hoped. Marie was looking after her?

Lissa assured him that she had everything she wanted, which was ironic, she thought, as she replaced the receiver and went back to work.

It was partly true that work was a panacea. Somehow she got through the rest of the day without bursting into tears again. But the pain was there all the time, pushed away deep inside her, ready to attack, and the night passed in a haze of misery. A *coup de foudre* was about the worst thing that could happen to you—when the person you loved didn't love you.

By late afternoon on Tuesday she had worked her way all through Hugh's manual. She closed the final page to shut out the sight of his writing. Even his writing had the power to hurt like hell.

He had done a wonderful job on the manual. In less than a week, from knowing nothing at all about the new computer, it had become a friend. There would be much more she could learn, given the time. But she felt she had mastered all the basics, and would be able to use it with confidence in any straightforward business transactions. She wasn't surprised that Hugh had great hopes for his new 'baby'. The launch would be a thrilling time for the company. But she wouldn't be there to share it.

She switched off for the last time, laid the final print-out on top of her notebooks for Hugh to check when he returned. Then she wandered out through the side door and flopped down wearily into one of the white-painted iron chairs on the long patio, trying to make up her mind what to do next. Hugh had said he would probably be back on Wednesday—that was tomorrow. She wasn't sure whether she could bear to stay and see him again— see that cold, distant look on his face when they met. Perhaps she should arrange for a taxi to collect her early in the morning...

'Hi there, sweetheart.'

She turned her head to see Paul striding along the patio towards her. He looked on top of the world. He wore an open-neck shirt and his throat showed the golden tan which he somehow managed to retain all year round. His light brown hair had streaks of gold, which he certainly hadn't acquired in Scotland. He must have been spending time in a male beauty-parlour.

Lissa smiled, feeling her spirits rise a little. Paul really was incorrigible, but somehow he made her feel better. 'Where on earth did you spring from?' she said. 'I'm afraid Hugh isn't here.'

He dropped into a chair beside her. 'I haven't come to see Hugh, I've come to see you, my pretty Lissa. I was amazed to see you at the gallery the other night, and found out from Claude Delage where I could find you.'

He studied her face. 'You look fagged, my lovely; what's been happening to you, and what are you doing here?' He chuckled. 'If it's not an indiscreet question.'

'It's all your fault,' she said. 'If you hadn't pounced on me in the office that night and Hugh hadn't turned up and been horrible to me I wouldn't have fallen down the stairs and twisted my knee and he wouldn't have felt he ought to look after me because my parents were away and the house was let to visitors and I'd nowhere to go.'

Paul was staring at her in amazement as she gabbled through an edited version of the events of a fortnight ago.

'Well, blow me down! I know the blighter's strong on this responsibility lark, but you must have hit him between the eyes, sweetheart, for him to bring you home to Mother.'

Lissa sighed. 'Oh, it wasn't like that. He thought I'd be useful to him with some computer work he's been doing. But tell me why you're in Paris and not in Scotland?'

Paul stroked back his wavy fair hair smugly. 'You may not believe this, but you see before you a new star rising in the Hollywood firmament.'

It didn't take Lissa long to get the whole story from him. In a Scottish hotel he had met an American film team who had been shooting an updated version of *The Thirty-Nine Steps* on location. Paul had palled up with the director, who had spotted Paul's photogenic possibilities and given him a film test. It had ended in Paul being offered a part in the director's next film, which was being made in Hollywood and needed an English actor.

'Better than selling office desks, what?' He grinned. 'But I've got to get out of the Winchester set-up straight away. Hugh's been trying to buy out my share and get rid of me for years—we've never hit if off. So I came over to Paris to give him the good news. He's fixing it up with the solicitors and as soon as I get my hands on some of the lolly I'm off to sample the joys of LA.'

'Well, congratulations,' Lissa said. 'I'm glad for you, if that's what you want.'

'But you haven't heard the lot yet. Another big surprise. I'm going to get married.'

'No,' Lissa teased. 'I don't believe it.'

'It's true, cross my heart. The rake is a reformed character.'

'Anyone I know?' Lissa had met one or two of Paul's girlfriends.

'Maybe you do,' Paul said. 'Her name's Carolyn Blake and she's working at Claude Delage's gallery. I met her there again when I called in the other night. It shook me rigid, seeing her again, I'd no idea she was there. You see——' he paused, examining the beautifully manicured nails on his left hand '—Carolyn and I were pretty close a few years ago and then—well, you know how it is—things went wrong and we drifted apart.'

Lissa stared at him, thoughts spinning round in her mind. Things Monique had said, the way Hugh, with his protective attitude to Carolyn, hated Paul. 'You mean,' she said slowly, 'she was pregnant and you ditched her?'

Paul's fair, handsome face coloured darkly. 'I suppose you could put it like that. These things happen all the time,' he went on defensively. 'I did what I thought was fair. I gave her money to—to get things put right. Then I was away in the US on a sales trip for six months, and I suppose I thought no more about it.'

Lissa looked at him with disgust. 'That wasn't very admirable.' She was beginning to see things from Hugh's viewpoint. Paul wasn't the harmless playboy she had imagined.

'No, I know it wasn't. I've felt guilty about it— from time to time,' he added with a sheepish, schoolboy grin. 'But now I've been given a chance to make it up to her. When I saw her again the other night I was knocked for six—and she was too, as it turned out. Neither of us had forgotten what we had together.'

In a dazed voice Lissa said, 'You're going to marry Carolyn? But I thought—I thought she was in love with Hugh.'

He shook his head. 'She told me all about that. She's grateful to him, but the poor kid's so alone— so lacking in confidence—she needed somebody...'

Hm, thought Lissa, I wouldn't have said Carolyn was lacking in confidence. She remembered Monique saying, 'Carolyn's a very pushy girl and what she's looking for is marriage.' Now it seemed as if she was getting her wish, so everybody ought to be pleased. And Hugh? She just didn't know.

'Isn't it wonderful?' Paul enthused. 'She's so beautiful—twice as beautiful as before. She'll wow them in California. We're going to have a whale of a time together—that is if Hugh coughs up.' His face clouded for a moment. 'I think he will, but he might foul things up just for spite—he hates my guts.'

Lissa nodded. 'I know. I didn't know why, but I can understand now.' She was beginning to understand a lot of things.

They sat on the patio for over an hour and Paul did most of the talking—about himself and his exciting future, raving about how Carolyn would put up his stock in LA—'It goes down a treat if you've got a ravishing girl on your arm'—about his part in the new film.

It began to get dark and Lissa got up. 'Do you want a drink before you go?'

'Better not,' Paul said. 'I'm driving a hired car and I'd rather stay alive until the wedding.'

He laughed down at her and put both hands on her shoulders. 'I'm glad I came,' he said. 'We've been pals, haven't we, and I wanted you to know the score from me—not from Hugh.'

She nodded. 'I hope you'll be very happy,' she said.

'Thanks, Lissa. I'll send you a postcard from LA,' he said with a grin. He put his arms round her and kissed her on the mouth. 'That's the one we didn't get around to properly before. Bye, love, I'll see myself out, my car's round the front.'

She watched him go, as he strode away jauntily. At the corner he turned and saluted and she waved back. Then she sat down again in the dusk.

Paul and Carolyn! It seemed like a happy ending. They would suit each other very well, for a time at least. She could just imagine them in California together, soaking up the sun and the anything-goes lifestyle. Paul certainly wasn't cut out for the pressures of business.

It was almost dark now and Lissa had finally made up her mind what to do. She went into the kitchen and found Henri there, reading the paper. Marie was busy at the stove.

Lissa had prepared her request carefully, and then memorised it, using the dictionary and the phrase book. Modern languages hadn't been her best subject at school, but vague memories of French lessons remained.

She smiled at Henri. *'Si'il vous plaît, monsieur. Je veux aller à Charles de Gaulle aéroport en le matin——'* what was 'tomorrow'? Oh, yes— *demain '—demain à neuf heures. Voulez-vous ordonner un taxi pour moi, s'il vous plaît?'*

There, how was that? Henri had got to his feet, flapping the newspaper and launching himself into a torrent of words which meant nothing to Lissa. But it seemed to her that he had understood, because he was nodding and smiling.

'A neuf heures,' Lissa repeated carefully. Nine o'clock would give her time to be on her way before Hugh returned. *'Merci bien.'* She smiled at Henri and went to her room to phone Claude at the gallery for news of Monique.

The news was good. Claude sounded relieved, almost buoyant. Monique had had a good day and was much, much better. Now it was only a matter of time for her to make a complete recovery. Tomorrow, he said, he would come home for a bath and fresh clothes. He would see Lissa then. He expected that Hugh would return tomorrow as well.

Lissa made a pretence of eating the meal Marie brought her. Marie knew there was something wrong—she wouldn't be surprised at Lissa's lack of appetite. Afterwards she went into the bedroom and began to pack.

At nine o'clock next morning Lissa was sitting in the hall with her travelling bag beside her, waiting for the taxi.

Writing the note to Hugh had been almost the worst part. 'Thank you for being so kind to me and for the enjoyable outings in Paris, but I'm sure you will understand that I have to leave now. I have very much enjoyed the work on the computer and hope you will find my notes satisfactory. Good luck with the launch. Yours, Lissa.'

She got up and walked to the door, her nerves raw. Waiting was agony—she expected to see Hugh drive up any moment. Had Henri understood that she wanted a taxi for nine o'clock?

She would have to try to find out. Searching her mind for the French words, she set off towards the kitchen—and saw Hugh coming downstairs.

They met in the middle of the hall.

'Oh, hello,' said Lissa, digging her nails into her damp palms, 'I didn't hear you come in.'

'No?' he said politely. Nothing had changed. His face was expressionless. He seemed to be looking through her, rather than at her.

'Had a good trip?'

'Very satisfactory, thank you.' His glance closed on her luggage beside the front door. 'You're leaving?'

She swallowed. 'We arranged Wednesday, didn't we? I've left a note for you in the office. I've worked right through the manual and I've left the print-out and some notes I've made.'

'Oh, yes?' he said distantly, not looking at her.

Suddenly desperate, she gulped, 'Is that all? No thanks for all my hard work? For the play-acting I put in on your behalf?' Play-acting, that was all it was, all it had ever been.

His eyes came down to hers and she saw how taut and strained his features were. He must have discovered that he loved Carolyn after all, now that Paul was going to marry her.

'Was it so very difficult?' he said wearily. 'Anyway, thanks.'

A screech of brakes outside on the gravel announced the arrival of the taxi.

He picked up her case and walked to the taxi with her. The driver took the case and stacked it in the back and held the door open.

'Goodbye, Hugh,' she said. She was dying slowly inside, trying to memorise every tiny detail of his face to take away with her. She started to hold out her hand but when he made no movement dropped it again. Her legs just about managed to climb into the taxi.

The driver slammed the door and got in behind the wheel.

Hugh had his hand on the door handle. 'I hope you've made the right decision,' he said, and stepped back as the taxi shot away down the drive. Lissa didn't look back. She knew that Hugh wouldn't be there.

The airport was colossal, crowded and terrifying. Remembering how Hugh had whisked her through it effortlessly on the way here, Lissa had a job not to sit down and dissolve into helpless tears. A hard lump seemed to have settled in her throat and she had to wait until she felt capable of speech. After pushing her trolley round for a time, she spotted a large desk marked 'Information' and made her way through the crowd towards it. Mercifully the girl on the other side of the desk spoke English.

Lissa explained her situation. 'I haven't enough French money but I've got a credit card—will that do? And how can I get a flight?'

The girl passed her on to a clerk at a desk further along the row. Here she learned that she could buy her ticket and be put on a 'wait-list' for the next flight to Heathrow. 'Oh, thank you,' Lissa breathed gratefully. At last something was going right. At last she would be getting away from this place where she'd been so happy—and so utterly, utterly miserable.

She opened her bag to get out her credit card and at the same moment a hand came from behind and gripped her arm. The bag flew out of her grasp and skidded across the ground. Her stomach twisted. Oh, no, not a mugging! Not now! Horrified, she spun round—to see Hugh stooping down to pick up her handbag.

'Sorry, Lissa,' he said calmly. 'Just wanted to stop you wasting your money on a ticket. Come on,' he said. He still had her arm in a firm grip, and with his other hand took hold of her trolley. 'I've had a hell of a job trying to find a parking spot. I just hope the car will be still there when we get to it.'

Lissa's knees felt weak and she could do nothing but go where he took her. They reached the car and he pushed her in unceremoniously. His face was expressionless as he started the car and drove in silence out of Paris with a recklessness she hadn't noticed about his driving before.

Reaching the house, he parked and switched off the engine. Lissa found her voice. 'What exactly is all this about?'

He led the way into the office and pointed to her notebook and the computer print-out she'd left behind. 'You made an utter botch-up of the spreadsheet,' he said. 'You left Mrs Smith with five hundred kilos of smoked salmon on her hands. She'd have been bankrupt, poor soul.'

Lissa's jaw dropped. 'Did I really? You've brought me back to tell me that?' She looked up and saw the way his grey eyes were sparkling with amusement.

He gave her a little push into the bedroom. 'We can talk here,' he said. 'Sit down.'

He settled himself in the only chair and Lissa sat on the edge of the bed and waited. To her utter amazement she saw that he was nervous. He cleared his throat and a pulse beat in his temple.

'So—you're not going to marry Paul?' he said.

She stared at him blankly. 'Of course I'm not going to marry Paul. Paul is going to marry Carolyn.'

'So I've just heard from Claude,' he said. 'I thought you and Paul . . . I must have got it wrong.'

She'd had enough of this—she wanted to hurt him the way she'd been hurt. 'Your precious logic deserted you at last?' she sneered.

He jumped up from his chair as if he'd been shot and grabbed her by the shoulders, shaking her—hard. 'Damn you, Lissa, it isn't funny. Do you mind terribly about Paul and Carolyn?'

'Stop it!' she screamed, tears spurting into her eyes. 'Stop it this moment.' He stopped shaking her and sank on to the bed beside her.

'What *is* all this about?' Her voice went up several semitones. 'Of course I don't mind, why on earth should I? Paul's nothing to me, never has been, except that I enjoyed working with him.'

'Then why did you let me think you were hooked on him?'

'I never did!' she shouted. 'It was you who kept on saying it. Over and over again. Paul—Paul—Paul. I got sick of denying it.'

He'd gone very pale. He sat beside her, not touching her, and said, quite calmly, 'Then if you're not going to marry Paul—would you consider marrying me?'

'*What?*' She couldn't have heard him right.

Suddenly his control wavered. 'Lissa, beautiful, adorable Lissa, you've got to marry me, because I want you for good and I can't go on without you. I love you, my darling, and I've never said those words before. It hit me like a rocket when I was in London—although I think I must have been in love with you right from the start—when you threw yourself down those stairs.'

'A *coup de foudre*?'

Hugh took both her hands and gazed into her eyes. 'Yes,' he said, 'a lightning strike. Although I didn't hear the thunder until you weren't there any more. All the time I was in London I nearly went crazy, thinking of you here, with Paul hovering. After that river trip—when we walked into the gallery and you saw him—I was watching your face—you looked like a girl in love. I was shattered, I wanted to kill the bastard.'

She drew in a long, shaky breath. 'I *was* in love,' she said. 'I am—with you.'

He drew away, staring at her in amazement. 'Say that again.'

'I love you,' she said recklessly. 'I've loved you for ages, ever since you bawled me out in the office that day. It was a *coup de foudre* with me too.' The tears welled into her eyes and ran down her cheeks. 'I love you and I want you, but you don't have to marry me. I know how you feel about marriage,' she ended up, choking a little.

'You don't know how I feel about marrying *you*,' he said, and the grey eyes were dark with passion. 'I'm going to enjoy showing you.'

His arms were around her and he was kissing her so fiercely she had to gasp for breath. One hand was on her thigh as he pushed her back on to the bed, stroking the softness through the gossamer stockings, working its way upwards beneath the flimsy underwear. He lifted his head, looking down into her eyes. 'You're not ...?'

'A virgin?' she said bravely. She shook her head. 'Once, after a college dance—it wasn't a great success ... Oh ...' She gasped as his fingers found the place they were searching for.

'Let's not waste any more time,' Hugh said thickly, ripping off his shirt. He helped her to undress and laid her gently on the bed. Then he was beside her, the warmth of his body infinitely exciting. 'We nearly got here once before,' he breathed into her ear as her curls spread out over the pillow. 'I've thought about it ever since—longed for it. This time there won't be any interruptions. Oh, darling, you're so lovely—so desirable ...'

He rolled her beneath him, gazing down at her, his eyes loving every part of her. Then his mouth travelled the route his eyes had taken and as she melted into him a slow fire began to consume her. Her heart was beating in heavy strokes, all her body softening, opening to him as he began expertly to touch, to kiss, to rouse her to a gasping, mindless frenzy that made her clutch and writhe and cry out his name, her hands digging into the smooth dampness of his back.

Her fingers traced out every separate vertebra—there was no spare flesh on him anywhere. Then her hands spread out, cupping his hips, drawing them down closer until with a groan of pleasure he thrust into her and she felt a wild, surging joy that was somehow possession as well as being possessed.

She wanted it to last forever, the plunging ecstasy, but at last there was a taut pause before the heart-stopping climax took them both into a final convulsive spasm that died away at last, leaving Lissa lying drained and gasping and utterly, blissfully fulfilled.

They lay still in each other's arms and Lissa savoured with delight the way a miracle had happened. Such a short time ago she had left this house in the blackness of despair and now her life had suddenly become bright and shining, like a newly minted coin. She hoped she wasn't dreaming.

Hugh stirred and buried his mouth in her neck, and in the hours that followed he proved to her over and over again that she wasn't dreaming.

Some time in the afternoon they got up and, after a lengthy and highly enjoyable period spent sharing the shower, they finally dressed and wandered hand in hand into the kitchen.

Marie's knowing black eyes passed over them and she chuckled drily, no doubt recognising *l'amour* when she saw it. She carried a plate of pastries and a huge pot of tea out on to the patio and Hugh pulled two chairs close together while Lissa poured out the tea.

Hugh shook his head in disbelief. 'I still can't take it in how bloody stupid I've been.'

'Logic and reason let you down?' Lissa teased.

He leaned over and kissed her hand. 'OK, I deserve that. I was so sure you were still keen on Paul, everything seemed to point to it. Right from the beginning I knew I wanted you, but I'd got so used to the idea that I didn't want marriage. I planned to make you forget him and I thought I was winning. Then it all went wrong. First Paul turning up and then Maman being taken ill. For a long time we didn't know whether she was going to make it.'

He shuddered. 'Just sitting there waiting—hell, it was a nightmare.'

'She really is getting better, isn't she?' Lissa said. 'I so wanted to see her before I left, but there didn't seem any way...'

'She's going to be fine.' Hugh put his hand over hers. 'When we tell her about us it'll hasten her recovery by days. She's liked you from the first moment she saw you, my darling—who wouldn't?'

Lissa's green eyes danced. '*You* didn't.'

'It wasn't anything to do with you—I was livid with Paul,' he said. 'I'd seen the way he'd treated Carolyn and I'd no intention of letting him repeat the performance if there was anything I could do to prevent it.'

Lissa said slowly, 'Yes, I think I understand that now. He told me all about it when he was here. Perhaps he'll settle down at last. He seems to be really in love with Carolyn now he's seen her again—and she with him. He came here specially to tell me about it when you were away—he was over the moon.'

Hugh poured out a second cup of tea and gulped it down. 'I wasn't away. I came back early from London. I couldn't wait to get back to you. I'd gone over to see the lawyers and arrange about buying Paul out of the company—as he wanted— and I couldn't concentrate because all the time I was terrified of what he'd get up to with you when I was out of the way. So at the first possible moment I flew back and came here—and there you were in his arms and he was kissing you and the world became a black hell from that moment on.

'I felt like a zombie. It's amazing how ordinary life goes on even when you're dead inside. I drove back into Paris and went to the hospital to sit with Maman and talked to her quite sanely—at least I think I did, it's all rather a blur. Then, afterwards, I had to see Paul at his hotel and tell him the result of my interviews with the lawyers and the directors of our company. He smirked and said he needed some cash on the spot because he planned to get married straight away.'

Lissa's eyes widened. 'You thought...?'

'Yes.' Hugh's face was grim. 'Of course I thought it was you. I'd seen you in his arms not an hour before. How I got out of that hotel without killing him I'll never know.'

'Oh...' Lissa sighed. 'What a muddle it all was. He'd come to tell me about Carolyn—rave about her—and that kiss was only to say goodbye.'

There was a long silence. The sun was getting low and long shadows fell across the patio. Lissa shivered and Hugh leaned over between their two chairs and laid his face against hers. 'I've been idiotic, I know that now, picking up all the wrong clues, jumping to the wrong conclusions.'

Lissa grinned. 'Logic doesn't work all the time.'

'Too true—not where love is concerned,' he said ruefully. 'Love isn't logical—thank heaven,' he added fervently.

He pushed his chair back and drew her to her feet, holding her close as if he would never let her go. 'Now I'm going to make plans.' The grey eyes were lit with enthusiasm. 'We're going to the hospital first to tell Maman our news; Claude will be there about now, too. Then we'll get your parents on the phone and tell them. I can't wait to meet them. Will they like me, do you think?'

Doubt clouded his eyes for a moment. Then he cheered up again. 'After that, I'm going to take you out for the most spectacular dinner at the best restaurant in Paris.' He kissed her again. 'Think of all the lovely things ahead of us, sweetheart. I want to take you to Dorset and show you our place there. I've got a cottage by the sea—you can see how you like it—we could buy something else if you don't.'

'And I'll be there to see the launch of the micro,' Lissa put in. 'I hated the thought that I'd miss that. Especially as I seem to have left poor Mrs Smith with an awful lot of smoked salmon on her hands.' She began to giggle. 'You're sure you want to marry a girl who couldn't cope with a spreadsheet?' she asked wickedly.

Hugh didn't smile. He held her and looked down into her eyes, and his own eyes were so full of love and tenderness that she felt suddenly shy. 'I want to marry *you*,' he said, his voice deep and husky. 'I love you to distraction and I want to spend the rest of my life with you.'

A slow smile touched his mouth then, before it came down to hers. 'And it's going to be a hell of a long time before I begin to think about a spread-sheet again,' he said.

Next month's romances

Each month, you can choose from a world of variety in romance with Mills & Boon. These are the new titles to look out for next month. .

THE STEFANOS MARRIAGE Helen Bianchin

THE LAND OF MAYBE Sandra Field

THE THREAT OF LOVE Charlotte Lamb

NO REPRIEVE Susan Napier

SOMETHING FROM THE HEART Amanda Browning

MISSISSIPPI MISS Emma Goldrick

RANCHER'S BRIDE Jeanne Allan

A VINTAGE AFFAIR Elizabeth Barnes

JUNGLE LOVER Sally Heywood

ENDLESS SUMMER Angela Wells

INHERIT YOUR LOVE Sally Cook

WILD CHAMPAGNE Kate Kingston

PORTRAIT OF A STRANGER Helena Dawson

NOT HIS PROPERTY Edwina Shore

Available from Boots, Martins, John Menzies, W.H. Smith, Woolworths and other paperback stockists.

Also available from Reader Service, P.O. Box 236, Thornton Road, Croydon, Surrey CR9 3RU.

Readers in South Africa — write to:
Independent Book Services Pty, Postbag X3010, Randburg, 2125, S. Africa.

4 FREE
Romances
and 2 Free gifts
-just for you!

Now you can enjoy all the heartwarming emotions of true love for FREE! Discover the uncertainties and the heartbreak, the emotions and tenderness of the modern relationships found in Mills & Boon Romances.

We'll send you 4 captivating Romances as a free gift from Mills & Boon, plus the chance to have 6 Romances delivered to your door every single month.

Claim your FREE books and gifts overleaf.

An irresistible offer from Mills & Boon

Here's a personal invitation from Mills & Boon Reader Service, to become a regular reader of romance. To welcome you, we'd like you to have four books, a CUDDLY TEDDY and a special MYSTERY GIFT absolutely FREE.

Then each month you could look forward to receiving 6 more Brand New Romances, delivered to your door, post and packing free! Plus our Free newsletter featuring author news, competitions and special offers.

This invitation comes with no strings attached. You can cancel or suspend your subscription at any time, and still keep your free books and gifts.

Its so easy. Send no money now. Simply fill in the coupon below and post it to - **Mills & Boon Reader Service, FREEPOST, PO Box 236, Croydon, Surrey CR9 9EL**

- - - - - - - - - **NO STAMP REQUIRED** - - - - - -

Free Books Coupon

YES! Please rush me my 4 Free Romances and 2 Free Gifts! Please also reserve me a Reader Service Subscription. If I decide to subscribe I can look forward to receiving 6 brand new Romances each month for just £8.70 delivered direct to my door, post and packing is free. If I choose not to subscribe I shall write to you within 10 days - I can keep the books and gifts whatever I decide. I can cancel or suspend my subscription at any time. I am over 18.

Name Mrs/Miss/Ms/Mr _____ EP87R

Address _____

_____ Postcode _____

Signature _____

mps
MAILING
PREFERENCE
SERVICE